This was just the beginning . . .

A blast of cold air hit Willow when she opened the back door. Trixie dashed outside, then skidded to an abrupt halt in the middle of the yard and began to sniff the air.

Willow knew the reason for her dog's agitation—a neighborhood cat that often strayed into the yard. She stepped outside to shoo the cat away.

Low-riding clouds hovered in a leaden sky devoid of moon and stars. Willow squinted through the darkness and thought she saw the cat perched on the back fence. But as she moved forward, the animal became transformed into the head and shoulders of a shadowy figure that slithered over the fence and came stealthily toward her. . . .

ABOUT THE AUTHOR

Lizabeth Loghry has always been a mystery buff. She began to take creative writing classes more than ten years ago and decided to try her hand at a Gothic novel—which she sold five years later. Since then she has turned to the romantic suspense genre. *Shadow of Deceit* is her first book for Intrigue. Liz has four daughters and lives near Sacramento.

Shadow of Deceit

LIZABETH LOGHRY

Harlequin Books

TORONTO • NEW YORK • LONDON
AMSTERDAM • PARIS • SYDNEY • HAMBURG
STOCKHOLM • ATHENS • TOKYO • MILAN

For my guardian.
And for my mother,
Jimmy, Amber and Rhonda,
who knows why.

Harlequin Intrigue edition published March 1987

ISBN 0-373-22061-8

Chapter One

Despite its classic elegance, the Clayton ranch house had always struck Willow Laughlin as cold and austere. She had formed this opinion the first time her childhood friend, Cassandra Clayton, had brought her to the ranch at the age of ten. Now, at twenty-seven, in spite of numerous return visits, Willow found her feelings unchanged. If anything, the three-story house seemed even more cheerless without Cassie's vivacious personality to brighten it on this cool Saturday evening.

Cassie had died ignominiously in prison early that morning of a rapid-moving disease, with only Willow beside her. As she'd promised, Willow had journeyed to Reno to deliver a letter from Cassie to her family. She had handed it to Cassie's widowed father, Addison, moments before. Then she'd joined him, his son, Brad, his daughter, Jennifer, and a man named Steven Randall in the ornate living room.

A log crackled in the hearth of the marble fireplace, and silk draperies concealed the February darkness. As Addison began to read the letter, Willow leaned back against the brocade sofa on which she sat. She was bone weary from her all-night vigil at Cassie's bedside, and deeply saddened by the loss of her best friend. Though six months had passed since Cassie's sensational trial for armored-car robbery, Willow was still shocked at her participation. Cassie and a man who'd later died during a prison riot had been caught and sentenced to twenty years each. But a third, unknown accomplice remained at large, and the two million dollars of bank money taken in the robbery hadn't been recovered.

Cassie had possessed a wild streak that often resulted in daring, sometimes dangerous exploits. Her excursion into crime surpassed anything she had ever done. The press, labeling her a madcap socialite and thrill seeker, had played up her involvement and treated it as a lark. But Willow knew there had always been a great deal of conflict between Cassie and her father, and that many of her escapades had been designed to punish him and ruin his reputation, as well. For although Addison projected a mild-mannered, easygoing image to the outside world, Willow was aware that he was dictatorial and manipulative toward his children. Especially Cassie.

Willow was so immersed in her thoughts that she didn't realize Jennifer had spoken to her. "I'm sorry. Did you say something to me?" She smiled at the blond, blue-eyed twenty-year-old, who closely resembled the rest of her family.

"I just wondered if you were ready for some coffee yet." Jennifer gestured toward the silver service that rested on a carved rosewood table in front of the sofa. But Willow had drunk gallons of coffee during the night and was sure she would float away if she had one more cup. She demurred with a smile, noting the lines of sadness etched in Jennifer's features. Brad's expression mirrored that of his younger sister as he sat near the fire in a wing chair, seemingly lost in his own reflections.

Though Willow had visited Cassie often in prison, and they'd kept in touch before that, she hadn't seen Brad, Jennifer or Addison for years. She knew Brad had gotten married a couple of years before, but recalled Cassie's having mentioned something about a recent separation. At thirty years old, Brad was good-looking in a boyish way, while Jennifer had been transformed from a gangly teenager into a tall, long-legged beauty.

As for Addison, he was still a big man and hadn't changed, except that his hair was almost completely silver. Willow hoped that now Cassie was gone, he would put behind him the bitter memories of their stormy relationship. She glanced at him to gauge his reaction to Cassie's letter. According to what Cassie had told her, it was simply a farewell message. Addison read it slowly, carefully, as if to catch the nuance of every phrase. A myriad of emotions flitted across his fleshy face, then disappeared as if abruptly erased. Willow sighed and focused her smoky gaze on Steven Randall, who sat at the other end of the sofa.

Brad had introduced him as Cassie's friend. Willow was sure, however, that Cassie had never mentioned him—which seemed odd, because she'd always talked freely about her various relationships, particularly those involving handsome men, a category which Steven Randall certainly fitted into. Well over six feet, he appeared to be in his early thirties, with

brown hair, ebony eyes and a slightly crooked nose
that looked as if it had been broken. His square chin
had a cleft, his bronzed skin declared him the out-
door type, and his dark trousers and tweed blazer
complemented his lithe but sinewy physique.

As though aware that Willow was looking at him,
Steven Randall set his cup and saucer on the coffee
table and turned to her with a smile. She smiled back
politely, then transferred her attention to Addison.
Having finished reading Cassie's letter, he rose and
almost flung it at Brad, intense disappointment
stamped in his expression. Then, instead of resuming
his seat, he prowled the spacious room and muttered
a string of curses under his breath.

Steven Randall continued to look at Willow
Laughlin. His glance took in the perfect oval face, the
long black hair that curled around the shoulders of the
white turtleneck sweater she wore with beige twill
slacks. She had a slender but curvaceous figure he
imagined brought out the vicious cat in other women.
Steven studied her a moment more before shifting his
gaze to Jennifer. "Mind if I smoke?" She said no; he
lit a cigarette, inhaled deeply, and watched as Addison Clayton came to an abrupt halt in front of the
object of Steven's former study.

"During the time you were with Cassie last night
and this morning, did she say anything about the armored-car robbery money?" Addison spoke with a
sense of urgency, as if Willow's reply were of the ut-
most importance. From certain things Cassie had said,
Willow thought she knew why.

Aside from being one of the wealthiest cattle
ranchers in Nevada, Addison had political aspira-

tions. He'd been running for governor of the state but
had withdrawn from the race because of adverse publicity surrounding Cassie's involvement in the crime.
An aura of scandal had hung over the Clayton name
ever since. Addison evidently felt that the recovery of
the money would not only restore his family honor but
also would ultimately enable him to reenter politics.

Since Willow was the last person to have spoken to
Cassie, she'd assumed that she would be questioned
about the missing money. The only thing she hadn't
anticipated was how swiftly word of Cassie's demise
would spread. An FBI agent had interrogated her
moments after Cassie had been pronounced dead. The
press, too, had obviously gotten wind of it, because
newspaper reporters had interviewed Willow as she left
the Federal Correctional Institution in Northern California, where Cassie had been incarcerated. And
she'd been waylaid yet again by the news media on her
arrival at the ranch.

In response to Addison's question, Willow answered, "No. She made no reference to it whatso-
ever."

Willow knew that Cassie had felt remorseful for her
part in the robbery, even though she'd steadfastly re-
frained from talking about it or the money. And despite her accomplice's having maintained that Cassie
knew where the money was, Willow was convinced
he'd lied. Addison apparently believed it was Cassie
who had withheld the truth, and his disgruntled scowl
showed that he was not satisfied with Willow's reply.

"If Cassie didn't say anything about the money,
what *did* she talk about? Try and remember. Even the
smallest detail could be important," he persisted, his

booming baritone rising, as though with increasing frustration. He watched Willow closely, his attitude imposing, and she wondered if he was trying to gain the information he sought through intimidation.

Beginning to feel like a witness under cross-examination, Willow went over the long night in her mind. She noted that Brad had risen to pass Cassie's letter to Jennifer, who started to cry quietly. Brad studied Willow as intently as his father was doing, while Steven Randall casually blew smoke rings into the air.

"As I told you before," Willow said to Addison, "Cassie was heavily sedated and drifted in and out of consciousness a lot. She talked about the special times of her childhood—Christmas, birthday parties, that sort of thing. That's really about all."

Willow recalled Cassie's having referred a couple of times to a surprise. But she'd assumed it was part of her rambling about the past, and saw no point in bringing it up now. Cassie had slipped into a final coma soon after, so Willow had no idea of what the surprise was, anyway.

Addison continued to tower over her. He opened his mouth as if to pursue the subject of her last conversation with Cassie, then stalked back to his chair.

Jennifer had finished reading the letter. She returned it to its envelope and murmured brokenly, "Poor Cassie... We should have been with her when..." She turned on Addison with uncharacteristic anger. "It's your fault we weren't! If you hadn't harassed her about that damned money, she'd have wanted us there..."

Addison rounded on her, his face purple with rage. "Control yourself or leave the room! I don't need you to tell me how I should or shouldn't have acted! Who the hell do you think you are to speak to *me* like that!"

"Would you like Ms. Laughlin and me to leave?" Steven Randall jumped into the fray, embarrassment written across his face. He crushed out his cigarette in a nearby ashtray and stood up.

"That won't be necessary. My daughter has nothing more to say. Have you, Jennifer?" Addison glared at her, his expression challenging and intimidating at the same time.

Both had the effect of quelling Jennifer's anger. "No. I didn't mean to... I'm sorry...." Her face scarlet, she rushed from the room, leaving an uncomfortable silence in her wake.

Addison's color was beginning to return to normal, but Willow knew that Jennifer was right about his treatment of Cassie. He had paid for the best defense attorneys during her trial and had visited her in prison on a regular basis, but he'd nagged her incessantly about the location of the money. Cassie had become so fed up with his constant harangues that she'd asked only for Willow when she knew the end was near.

The prolonged pause that followed Jennifer's departure threatened to stretch into infinity. As though to relieve the tension, Brad turned to Willow. "Cassie's body is being brought home in a few days for private interment; not even the family will be present. But her memorial service is slated for tomorrow afternoon. I'm sure she would want you there, and it seems senseless for you to go home and come back again tomorrow. Why not spend the night here instead?''

From the censorious inflection in Brad's tone, Willow gained the impression that he disapproved of Cassie's private interment. She surmised, as well, that it was Addison who had made the decision. By letting Cassie go alone to her grave, he was extracting final revenge for the havoc she had created in his life.

Willow pushed the thought aside and considered Brad's suggestion. At this point, the half-hour drive to her home in Carson City loomed before her as an endless journey. When Addison confirmed the invitation, she accepted.

Brad smiled his approval. ''Dinner's in an hour or so. You'll probably want to freshen up first. I'll have someone show you to one of the guest rooms.'' He moved to tug a brocade bell pull in a corner.

Presently, the Claytons' cook-housekeeper, Opal Andrews, entered the room. The plump middle-aged woman had become a surrogate mother to Addison's children with the passing of his wife when Jennifer was born. Opal glanced around at the group, then, spotting Willow, greeted her as an old friend.

''Miss Willow, it's been ages since I saw you here! How have you been?''

Willow warmly returned Opal's greeting and got to her feet when Brad told Opal to direct Willow to a room on the second floor.

Before the two left the living room, he asked Willow if she had brought any luggage. She mentioned the small pullman case in her car, and he promised to send somebody up with it. As Willow followed Opal into the hall and up a flight of marble stairs, the older woman brought up the subject of Cassie.

"Jennifer told me you were with her at the last. I'm so glad; our darling Cassie always thought the world of you."

"And I her," Willow assured Opal.

They moved to the upper landing and started down a long corridor whose series of rooms made up the family wing. Opal opened a door near the end and flicked the wall switch.

Her critical glance swept over the white French provincial furniture, the high-gloss hardwood floor, the original paintings that adorned the silk-covered walls. The suite was as elegant as the rest of the house. Her inspection completed, Opal commented sympathetically, "You poor little thing. You look completely done in. You've time to lie down for a while before supper, if you like."

The bed beckoned invitingly, but Willow had worn the same clothing for almost twenty-four hours and felt positively grubby. She longed for a bath and told Opal as much. After checking the adjacent bathroom for clean towels and washcloths, the housekeeper said, "Your things should be along directly. But if you need anything, just use that." She nodded toward a bell pull near the window and closed the door softly behind her.

Soon after, a young maid brought Willow's suitcase. As Willow surveyed its contents, she gave an impatient sigh. When she'd received the phone call from the prison authorities summoning her, she had assumed she would be gone overnight and had packed the necessary toiletries, nightgown, slippers, robe and a skirt and blouse. The skirt was brown wool, the blouse cream-colored silk, both of which would be fine under ordinary circumstances. Willow remembered from past visits, however, that the Claytons dressed formally for their evening meal. Since there was nothing she could do about it, she asked the maid to press the skirt and blouse.

After a leisurely bath, Willow got dressed and descended the stairs to the living room, where everyone was having cocktails. As she'd expected, the Claytons were formally attired. Only Steven Randall hadn't changed, and his casual appearance made Willow feel better. Although Jennifer seemed to be in control of herself now, her pretty face contained the visible remnants of her earlier emotional stress. To Willow's surprise, Addison had apparently overcome his former frustration. He was really quite cordial when he turned from a serving cart, which held assorted cocktail ingredients, and spied her. "Ah, Willow. There you are. What's your pleasure?"

"Oh, just a soft drink, please." She was afraid that alcohol would heighten her exhaustion and put her literally under the table.

Addison handed her a glass of cola, just as a maid entered to announce that dinner was served.

In the dining room with its magnificent Waterford crystal chandelier, the three men discussed the cattle business, which Brad managed for Addison. Jennifer contributed nothing to the discussion, and since cattle raising was a subject foreign to Willow, she merely listened politely. She hadn't eaten since breakfast and tucked into the meal with relish, but paused with a forkful of succulent roast beef halfway to her mouth when she encountered Steven Randall's gaze.

He was scrutinizing her intently across the table, his eyes narrowed in speculation. It was as if he were trying to decide something about her, and there was an element in his penetrating scrutiny that made Willow suddenly uneasy. To conceal her discomfort, she kept on eating.

Steven hadn't realized he was staring at Willow Laughlin until he caught her reproving look. Not that it mattered. She couldn't read his thoughts, which was probably a good thing; he didn't think she'd like them. He wrested his glance from her and took a sip of the excellent Cabernet Sauvignon that accompanied the meal.

The men continued to talk about cattle for a time. Then, in an obvious attempt to draw Willow into the conversation, Addison said, "If I remember right, the last time I saw you, you'd gotten a job as a court reporter. Are you still doing that? How long has it been since I've seen you, anyway? Must be two, three years, at least."

"It's been five, actually." Willow looked at him, surprise in her gray eyes. While Addison had never been exactly rude to her, he hadn't actively singled her out for conversation, either. At the moment, he seemed to be making a special effort to be nice to her, and she wondered if he felt guilty for having interrogated her about her final visit with Cassie. He'd never seemed the sort of man who would feel regret for anything he did, but she decided to give him the benefit of the doubt.

"I imagine you meet people from all walks of life in that type of work. It must be interesting." Steven Randall broke into Willow's musings, the smile he gave her bringing the cleft in his chin into prominence.

She agreed that it was. Then, when Addison suggested coffee and brandy in the living room, she excused herself and went up to her room. She was exhausted.

Willow felt certain she would fall asleep as soon as her head touched the pillow. But once she was in bed, the events of the past twenty-four hours began to parade through her head. She still found it remarkably odd that Cassie had never mentioned Steven Randall and wondered whether they had simply been friends or something more, or whether Cassie had perhaps found it necessary to keep their relationship secret, and if so, what her reason could have been.

The various possibilities sent thoughts tumbling through Willow's head like a tumbleweed in the strong Nevada wind, and though she was now so exhausted that she ached, she couldn't turn her brain off. She lay for more than an hour staring into the darkness. Then, thinking that something to read might relax her enough to sleep, she got out of bed, switched on the light, shrugged herself into her robe and started downstairs to the library.

Normally she would have asked permission to borrow a book, but she guessed from the heavy silence that met her that the others had gone to their rooms. Even the servants seemed to have turned in for the night. She wondered if Steven Randall was also staying in the house, but dismissed him from her thoughts as she entered the library.

The pleasant scent of leather emanated from floor-to-ceiling shelves, some of which held an impressive collection of well-bound first editions. She spotted several of the Dickens novels that were among her favorites, but passed these over to select a Regency romance novel. In the hope that the light material would lull her into sleep, she carried it to her room.

Willow was closing the bedroom door when her glance happened to stray to the velvet-upholstered bench near the window on which her luggage rested. She hesitated with her hand on the knob. She had neatly folded and arranged the contents of her case after preparing for bed, but now one leg of her panty hose stuck out like a ghostly, transparent limb.

She set the book aside and raised the lid of the suitcase. Everything inside lay in a tangled heap. Her makeup kit had been opened, as well. Containers of eye shadow were strewn all over her clothes, and her lacy slip bore smudges of blue, silver and gold. She was glad she'd hung up her skirt and blouse in the closet.

Her leather handbag was beside the case, and she looked through it to see if anything had been taken. Her cash, checkbook and credit cards were all there, and she saw no evidence of theft. Still, someone had obviously searched her luggage during her short absence. Willow stared down at the mess, suddenly outraged by this flagrant invasion of her privacy.

She reached out to gather up the eye shadow applicators but paused once more, her scalp tightening as the sensation of eyes boring into her back slithered

along her spine. In the next instant, outrage turned
into apprehension. It occurred to her that although she
had seen no one when she'd entered, she could not be
alone in the room. Whoever had searched her things
was concealed somewhere, watching her at this very
moment.

Chapter Two

No sooner had this disturbing thought struck than Willow heard a creaking sound. As if weight had been shifted or as if a foot had surreptitiously been moved.

The noise seemed to have come from behind her, from the area near the door. She instinctively started to turn, and at the same time she discerned a rushing movement. Then, instantaneously, the room was plunged into darkness. Willow's startled yelp was muffled by running footsteps as her unknown visitor beat a rapid retreat.

Her heart pounding, Willow remained where she was, too disoriented by the blinding darkness to move at first. Then, as anger replaced apprehension, she went after the intruder, determined to find out who it was.

She couldn't see her hand in front of her face, let alone make out where she was going. That became painfully clear when she stubbed her big toe on something hard in her path. From the shape of the obstruction, she guessed it was the leg of the bed, and her pain-filled "Damn!" exploded around her as she gingerly groped her way toward the door.

The dimly lit corridor was empty, and Willow halted, uncertain about what to do. She had no intention of letting the incident go unreported. Since Addison was the head of the house, she hobbled to his suite at the end of the hall. The silence that greeted her sharp-knuckled rap told her that he was either asleep or not there. Determined nonetheless to relate the episode to someone, Willow went first to Brad's room, then to Jennifer's. Again she received no response and was left with no choice but to wait until morning.

To prevent any more nasty surprises, however, she took the precaution of locking the door to her own room before she crawled back into bed. She felt sure that the searcher had hidden behind the door. Hence, that eerie feeling of eyes drilling into her back. But who had it been? What had he or she been looking for?

Steven Randall immediately came to mind, probably because he was the only stranger there. Also, Willow couldn't connect the Claytons with such sneaky behavior. Addison, perhaps, she amended. She had always thought him capable of doing just about anything he considered necessary to reach a goal. But then she recalled the newspaper reporters she had spoken to on her arrival at the ranch. She'd told them only that she was there to deliver something from Cassie to her family. She wondered now, though, if one of them had gained entry and gone through her possessions, seeking a story.

But would a member of the press have known which room she was using? She didn't think so. Yet nothing else made any sense.

THERE WAS NO SIGN of Addison or Brad when Willow came downstairs the next morning, but Jennifer was in the breakfast room adjacent to the kitchen. She ate with good appetite today and seemed in a talkative mood. She told Willow about the courses she was taking at the University of Nevada, where she was majoring in interior design. Willow still intended to tell someone about the previous night's episode, preferably Addison, but Jennifer said that he and Brad were taking care of ranch business and weren't expected back until later. So Willow told her instead.

"You're kidding!" Jennifer exclaimed, incensed. "Who'd want to do that, and why, for heaven's sake?"

"I don't know for sure, but I *think* I have a good idea."

Willow related her suspicion about an overeager newspaper reporter, and Jennifer retorted, "I can believe that. Thanks to the press, this whole thing with Cassie has been a three-ring circus from the start. They were always hounding her for an interview, wanting to know what life was like for her behind prison bars. God! Will it ever stop?"

Willow reached across the table to give Jennifer's hand a reassuring squeeze. "Let's hope it'll be over after today." Even as she spoke, she was filled with a sudden feeling that the opposite was true, that something that would touch her life in some indefinable way had only just begun. The feeling was an unreasonable one, and Willow quickly shook it off. After breakfast, at Jennifer's suggestion, she accompanied her on a long walk around the vast grounds.

Willow saw nothing of Steven Randall during the day and wondered if he planned to attend Cassie's memorial service. She put the question to Brad as he drove her and Jennifer in his Mercedes sedan through the snow-banked streets to the chapel where the service was to be held. Addison, accompanied by two relatives who had arrived after lunch, rode ahead in a chauffeur-driven limousine.

"I doubt it," Brad said. "He took off sometime last night." Brad lapsed into silence as if he had other things on his mind, and the three remained quiet for the rest of the drive.

Cassie's memorial service was solemn and concise. Brad turned out to be correct. Randall wasn't among the mourners, the ever-present press or the curiosity seekers who lined the sidewalk as everyone filed out of the chapel when the brief ceremony ended. The man's absence seemed almost as odd as Cassie's having omitted to mention their friendship.

Soon after they got back to the ranch, Willow thanked Cassie's family for their hospitality, said her goodbyes, then drove away. Moments later she was heading south toward Carson City, her late-model Camaro hungrily chewing up the miles. Cattle ranches flanked the two-lane highway, and the sagebrush, creosote and greasewood bushes that studded the snow-blanketed terrain grew sparse as she neared town. After sweeping past motels, casinos and wedding chapels, she turned down a street near the courthouse where she worked, then eased the car to a stop in the driveway of a brick-fronted house on the corner of the block.

Once inside, Willow set her things down on a rust-colored wing chair that complemented the ruffle-shaded lamps that made up the Early American decor. Her salary, as well as the private depositions she did for various attorneys, had enabled her to buy the two-bedroom house a couple of years before.

In spite of having risen late, she was still tired from lack of sleep, and was tempted to prop up her feet and relax a while. But she had left Trixie, her cockapoo, with her next-door neighbor and knew the dog would be anxious to get home.

The wail of a siren on nearby North Carson Street drifted toward Willow as she went up the narrow cement walkway to Eileen Sutton's front porch. She'd telephoned her during the morning to explain that she had spent the night at the ranch, and Eileen had told her to take her time getting back. As she opened the door now, Eileen greeted Willow with a cheery "Hi, lady. Glad you made it back okay." She led the way into the living room.

Eileen had rented the house shortly after Cassie's conviction, and she and Willow had developed an instant rapport. A year or so older than Willow, Eileen taught physical education at a local high school. She was tall with a rounded figure she kept in shape by playing tennis and swimming. Her fawn-colored hair was naturally sun streaked, and her hazel eyes contained a perpetual gleam of optimism.

Willow sat down and scanned the room for Trixie. As if in reply to her unspoken question, Eileen smiled. "Mike's puttering around in the garage, and Trixie's with him." Eileen's husky voice softened at the mention of her live-in boyfriend, Mike Peters, but took on an inquisitive note when she turned the topic to Willow's last visit with Cassie.

"It must have been a grim ordeal for you, poor baby. Feel like talking about it?"

Willow agreed that it had, indeed, been grim. But she realized with wry amusement that her friend would probably burst with frustrated curiosity if she said no. Eileen had always been impressed by Willow's relationship with one of the state's wealthiest socialites. She was also inordinately intrigued with Cassie's luxurious life-style and her venture into crime—so much so that each time Willow had gone to see Cassie in prison, she knew that she would be quizzed by Eileen about every detail of the visit.

Willow gave Eileen a full account of her final time with Cassie. She mentioned that Cassie's family had not been there at the end.

"So you don't know how they took the news of her death when they found out?" Eileen's hazel eyes gleamed with an inquisitive light. "What about Cassie's father? You always said there was bad blood between them. Did he finally mellow toward her?"

"Well, I'm sure Cassie's sister and brother felt bad. But with Addison, it's hard to tell. He *was* her father, for goodness' sake, so he must have felt something. But his attitude was anything but mellow. He seemed mad as hell, in fact, about the letter Cassie left. He—"

"That's right," Eileen cut in. "You mentioned something on the phone about a letter. That must've been sad for her family, knowing it was probably the last thing she ever wrote. Did you read it?"

"No. According to Cassie, it was essentially a goodbye message. But Addison evidently hoped the letter explained where the armored-car robbery money was. I think he thought she might have said something to me about it, too. He really gave me the third degree." Willow frowned in remembered annoyance.

Just then the back door opened and a small white whirlwind bounded into the room. Trixie spied Willow, leaped into her lap and smothered her face with wet kisses.

"I know, you missed me; I missed you, too." Willow laughed as she fondly stroked the dog.

"So you came back after all," Mike Peters remarked, advancing into the room. His loose-limbed stride was in perfect harmony with his lanky physique.

"Did you doubt I would?" Willow asked, returning his friendly grin.

Mike shed his jacket and sat beside Eileen on the sofa. "Sort of. Eileen said you'd spent the night with your rich friend's relatives. I thought you'd like the taste of luxury so much that you'd decide to stay. Or maybe even head for Hollywood—you're getting to be such a celebrity around here. There was a snapshot in last night's paper of you leaving that prison where your friend was. Didn't do you justice, though. You're a heck of a lot prettier than that." Mike sent her a wolfish look, a playful grin crinkling the corners of his tawny eyes.

"I didn't know that. About my picture being in the paper, I mean. But thanks for the compliment." Willow smiled, unsurprised to hear that she'd been in the newspaper again. Since she was Cassie's best friend, the press had contacted her on several occasions for information. Willow had even been mentioned in a local magazine article, which reported Cassie's illness. Afterward she had the dubious distinction of having been recognized by a clerk in a grocery store. It was a distinction she would have gladly done without, and she hoped that her life would assume some semblance of normalcy from now on.

Willow voiced her feelings. And Mike murmured, his angular face serious, ''Yeah. You know I like to tease you about getting your picture in the papers. But I can see where being bugged by the news media would get old after a while.'' His hair was tousled from the stiff breeze outside, and he ran a smoothing hand through the short sandy strands.

Mike was a couple of years older than Eileen. He sold new cars for a dealership in town. The two women had met him at a disco where they sometimes went to dance, and he and Eileen had started dating soon after. Willow knew her friend was serious about Mike, and assumed from his having moved in with her that he felt the same way.

Since she liked Mike, she was pleased for Eileen. As for herself, Willow had recently ended her relationship with an attorney with whom she'd fallen impetuously in love. He'd been so witty, sophisticated and charming that within a week of their first meeting, she'd felt certain she'd found her ideal man. His own declaration of love had seemed completely sincere. She'd discovered what a consummate liar he really was, however, when she learned from a mutual friend that he was seeing at least two other women besides her.

The knowledge that she had been so easily deceived rankled even now. But at the same time it strengthened her determination to take any future romantic relationship at a much slower pace.

ON THE FOLLOWING MONDAY, eight days after Cassie's memorial service, Willow went to work prepared for a lengthy courtroom session. On the first day of a criminal trial, each potential juror was questioned repetitiously by the attorneys, and Willow had to take everything down on her stenograph machine. Although she enjoyed her profession, this aspect of it was monotonous. The work required such intense concentration that she was only distantly aware of the courtroom door opening sometime later and of someone taking a seat among the spectators. Not until the judge called the lunch recess did she glance up from her machine to see Steven Randall striding toward her.

Willow stared at him in surprise, wondering what he was doing there. As if to explain, he approached with a smile and said, "Hi. I was across the street at the bank when I remembered you worked here. I thought I'd come over and ask you to lunch. That is, if you haven't already made other plans."

As he came to stand beside her, Willow realized she had forgotten how tall he was in comparison to her five feet four inches, and how attractive. Nor, she guessed, was she the only one who noticed. Several female jurors paused to look at him as they filed out of the courtroom, their admiring glances roaming over the tan leather jacket, brown slacks and white shirt that fitted his athletic frame as if they had been hand-tailored for him.

"Well, I . . . uh . . . no, I haven't." The surprise of seeing Steven Randall again caused Willow to stammer, and she felt an unaccustomed flush steal over her face. To cover her embarrassment, she studied the toe of her gray pumps, then brushed back an imaginary stray lock of her French-plaited hair.

Steven noticed the color that stained her cheeks, the self-conscious gesture she made with her hair. He wondered if these were devices she used to create an impression of demure innocence, which turned some men on. If so, she was wasting her talent. Those tricks, along with a few others, had been tried on him so many times that he was immune to them. His mouth curved in a sardonic twist, which he quickly turned into an encouraging grin when Willow glanced up at him.

Even though she hadn't thought of Steven since they had met at the Clayton ranch, Willow was still curious about his relationship with Cassie. She decided to accept his invitation. She usually had lunch at home, and recalling the fried chicken she planned to have, she invited him to share it.

They arranged to meet on the front steps of the courthouse, where he was waiting when Willow emerged from the building five minutes later.

The state capitol lay across from the courthouse. Steven appeared to be studying the domed structure, but his expression was preoccupied, remote, as if he were miles away. From the intense frown that furrowed his high forehead, Willow guessed that his thoughts were unpleasant.

Steven seemed so absorbed in his reflections that she had to ask him twice if he was ready to go. When he finally acknowledged her question, he did so distractedly. "What . . . ? Oh, sure thing. . . ."

With the reply, he gave Willow a penetrating look of speculation similar to that which he had given her at the Clayton ranch. It made her decidedly uneasy, although she could not have said why. She started to comment on that probing scrutiny, but Steven walked down the steps, leaving her with the unspoken words hanging on her lips.

North Carson Street teemed with noon-hour traffic as Steven and Willow walked the four blocks to her house. The cold crisp air was invigorating after the stuffiness of the overheated courtroom. Steven filled his lungs with it, a satisfied grin curving his mouth as he gave Willow a covert glance. He had known the importance of making contact with her and secretly congratulated himself on how easily it had been accomplished.

In the entry hall, Trixie greeted Willow with her usual unrestrained exuberance. She danced around Willow's feet, and her excited barking drowned out the sound of the television coming from the living room.

"Well, hello there. Who's this little fella?" Steven squatted to stroke the dog's velvety head. Trixie's attitude toward the stranger was curious but reserved at first. Then, accepting him as a new friend, she licked his outstretched hand, and her tail became a white flag in perpetual motion.

Though Steven was a foot or so away, Willow could smell the spicy scent of his after-shave. It mingled with the tobacco he smoked to make a surprisingly pleasant combination. She sniffed appreciatively as she corrected him. "It isn't a he; it's a she. Her name's Trixie."

Trixie rubbed herself against Steven's legs when he stood up, a definite sign of approval. As Willow showed him into the living room, she recalled wryly that Trixie had taken just as quickly to the attorney with whom she had been involved.

Steven's interested glance traveled around the room. It paused on the television and the lamps, which glowed brightly on the maple accent tables near the sofa. "Do you always go away and leave everything on?"

"Only a couple of lights and the TV. Trixie doesn't like being by herself, and I leave them on so she won't get lonely. Her favorite programs are the daytime soaps. She never misses them," Willow joked as she led her unexpected guest into the kitchen, where she let Trixie out into the backyard.

Over the chicken, a crisp green salad, rolls and coffee, Willow and Steven got acquainted. She smiled at him over the vase of yellow silk roses that decorated the table and asked him what he did for a living. They had already established the fact that neither was married.

Steven buttered a roll as he smiled back. "I sell real estate. At the moment, I'm in the midst of moving here from Reno. I'd been there for quite a while and got into a rut, so I decided to pull up stakes and go somewhere else."

Willow had moved from Reno to Carson City herself five years before when she had started her present job and her parents and younger brother had moved to Oregon. Although she liked the city well enough, it was small, quiet, the life-style sedate. It seemed a peculiar place for him to have chosen to get out of a rut. She started to point this out, but Steven continued. "I just bought a condo on the south side of town. I'll be moving in soon and starting a new job with Nationwide Realty Company." As he spoke, he lifted his coffee mug to his mouth, and Willow noticed the large horseshoe-shaped diamond ring he wore on the little finger of his right hand. It looked expensive, as did his clothes, and she assumed that the real estate business was a lucrative one.

Yet his job came as a surprise. Willow would never have connected him with that type of work. Not that there was anything wrong with being a real estate agent, but his dark good looks, the vitality he exuded even while doing something as passive as sitting, brought to mind far more exciting professions—race car driver, international spy, master jewel thief.

Willow picked up a drumstick and bit into it. Steven paused as he wiped his mouth with his napkin, his attention suddenly riveted on her. There was something sensuous in the way her small, even teeth stripped the meat from the bone, and he found himself watching her with reluctant fascination. She wasn't only bright and beautiful, but she could cook, too. The batter on the deep-fried chicken was the best he'd tasted in years. But he reminded himself that he wasn't there for the food or the lady's company. So when he saw Willow looking at him with a question in her eyes, he asked her to pass the salt.

"Not that everything isn't great. I'm just an addict, I guess." His apologetic grin tilted the corners of his mouth and emphasized the cleft in his chin.

Willow offered him the salt shaker, wondering amusedly if he was aware that to lace his food with salt was a slur on the cook's skills, and got up to answer Trixie's insistent scratching on the door.

As Willow sat down at the table again, she belatedly recalled Steven's absence from Cassie's memorial service. In reply to her comment, he said, "I'd planned to go, naturally. But I was called away unexpectedly and couldn't make it back in time."

"I know you and Cassie were friends, but it's funny, I don't remember her ever mentioning you. How did you two meet? Had you known each other long?"

Willow heard the interrogative note that crept into her voice, but Steven evidently hadn't. "She probably didn't think I was important enough to mention," he responded ruefully, "much as I hate to admit it. We met about a year and a half ago in Carmel. Cassie threw a party at the Claytons' summer home there, and I went with a buddy of mine who knew her. She and I hit it off so well that we became good friends."

As if he could read her mind, Steven added wryly, "Cassie's and my friendship was strictly platonic, in case you're interested."

The man wasn't only perceptive, but he also had a disconcerting way about him that Willow wasn't sure she liked. Nor was she satisfied with his glossed-over explanation about why he thought Cassie had never spoken of him.

"Speaking of Cassie, I seem to remember her telling me you two met at school," Steven remarked, interrupting Willow's thoughts.

Although Cassie had kept quiet about him, she'd apparently told Steven about Willow.

"That's right. It was a parochial school. We were in the fourth grade. I guess her father sent her there hoping the regimen would tame her wild streak."

"I've heard about some of Cassie's antics, of course," Steven said as he poured himself another cup of coffee from the carafe at his elbow. "I think everybody in the state of Nevada has. Is it really true that she showed up at a society costume ball dressed as Lady Godiva, riding a horse and wearing only a long wig?"

"Unfortunately, yes. I guess the press had a field day with that." Willow chuckled. "But that was mild compared with some of her other escapades. Like the time she and her family were vacationing in Spain, and she ran with the bulls at Pamplona."

"I thought that was restricted to males." Steven's expression showed open amusement.

"It is, but Cassie dressed like a boy and did it, anyway. That was one of her little capers that backfired. She was trampled by a bull and broke her arm, and the Spanish government was so incensed that she and her family were nearly thrown out of the country. Cassie told me later that she and Addison had had a terrible row the night before and she wanted to get back at him. A lot of the things she did were in retaliation for something he'd done to outrage her."

"It sounds childish and self-destructive, though. Kind of like cutting off her nose to spite her face,"

Steven observed. "Cassie was a lot of fun to be with, and I liked her a lot, but . . ."

The thought that Cassie had self-destructive tendencies had crossed Willow's mind more than once over the years, but the note of criticism she detected in Steven's tone seemed disloyal to her memory. Willow reacted defensively. "I don't know how well you know Addison, and I don't like knocking people, but Cassie had reason to resent him for the way he tried to run her life. And he did do that. To the point that when he disapproved of the man she married, he paid him to divorce her. It nearly broke her heart; she really loved the guy."

Aware of the annoyance that flashed in Willow's eyes, Steven gave her another apologetic smile. "Actually, I don't know Cassie's father all that well," he conceded. "But I get the impression you don't care very much for him."

"Let's just say that if he ever does run for governor, he won't get my vote. He was easier on Brad and Jennifer, probably because they've always knuckled under. But he was a real stinker to Cassie. That's enough about Addison, though. How about some dessert? I baked a German chocolate cake last night, so it's still fresh."

They went on to exchange information about their personal backgrounds. Willow learned that Steven had been born and raised in Arizona, and that he was an only child. At his prompting, she told him about her own family, then a while later, he walked her back to the courthouse.

As they stood briefly together on the front steps, Steven said, "When I get settled, I'll give you a call, if that's okay with you. Maybe we could have dinner sometime.''

It occurred to Willow once more that perhaps Cassie had had a reason for keeping her relationship with Steven secret. She was more than ever curious about that reason and thought that if she saw him again he might say something to indicate what it was. She agreed without hesitation.

"Good!" Steven approved before turning to stride down the steps. But no sooner had he rounded a corner and disappeared from sight than Willow was flooded with misgivings. Her instincts told her that there was more to this man than met the eye. Then, too, she found the intense way he scrutinized her wholly unsettling. Even now, as she opened the courthouse door and slipped inside, the memory produced such a strong sense of uneasiness in her that she suppressed a sudden shiver.

Chapter Three

This was Willow's week for the unexpected. A couple of days later, when she returned home from work, she found a large cardboard box on her front porch. Her mother always sent her a birthday gift, but her birthday wasn't until July, and since she hadn't ordered anything through the mail, she couldn't imagine what the box contained. She tried to read the postmark, but couldn't make it out in the dim porch light. The box was so heavy that she had to drag it inside.

Once she had got it into the living room, Willow could see that it bore the return address of the prison where Cassie had been. Curious, she went into the kitchen for a knife to cut through the thick tape that sealed the box.

Attached to an inside flap was a brief message from a Frank Fielding, who identified himself as head prison guard. Willow remembered having seen him several times when she'd visited Cassie. Fielding explained that the enclosed had been left in the craft shop of the prison, and a note found among Cassie's possessions, instructing that it should be forwarded to Willow Laughlin.

More curious by the second, she brushed away the Styrofoam packing, then carefully lifted out the contents. An astonished "Ohh" escaped her lips when she found a three-story Victorian dollhouse, complete with gingerbread around the eaves. The exterior was painted white, the shutters green and a white picket fence enclosed the front yard.

This must have been the surprise Cassie had mentioned before she died.

Cassie had given her a similar dollhouse for Christmas the year they had met. Willow had cherished the gift more than any she'd ever received, so she was heartbroken when it was destroyed in a fire her younger brother had started while playing with matches in her bedroom.

Willow set the new dollhouse on the coffee table to examine it, smiling at the irony of her brother's having become a fireman in Portland, Oregon.

A wide structure, slightly over two feet tall, the dollhouse boasted double doors at the rear, which could be opened and four rooms with vaulted ceilings. Carpeted stairs led to the two top floors. The uppermost, a sitting room, contained a tiny Franklin stove. The second floor was partitioned to make two rooms. A master bedroom held a mahogany four-poster bed, a mirrored dressing table with a flounced chintz skirt and a velvet chaise longue. Toiletries lined the top of the dressing table, and cabbage-rose wallpaper brightened the walls. The other room was a nursery with a solid mahogany cradle containing a baby snuggled under a blue afghan. A colorful carousel adorned the top of a chest of drawers, and a beautifully carved wooden rocking horse rested near the cradle.

Willow was enchanted. The largest room, a parlor on the first floor, was her favorite. It was a veritable treasure trove filled with all sorts of surprises. She smiled with delight when she raised the lid of a sewing table and found compartments holding miniature thimbles, thread, scissors and needles. A little man and woman, she doing embroidery, he reading a newspaper, had been placed on a velvet settee near a fireplace. A lacquered cabinet with etched-glass doors opened to reveal knickknacks and real jade figurines. A pie-crust table with wax fruit under a glass dome stood near the settee. A petit-point sampler and matching oval rug decorated the wainscotted wall and hardwood floor.

The furnishings had been glued in place so that they wouldn't scatter when the dollhouse was moved.

Although Willow loved the dollhouse and was deeply touched by Cassie's gesture, she was mystified why Cassie had given it to her. She peered into the discarded box to see if it contained anything else and, spying an envelope at the bottom, scooped it up and tore it open. It contained a letter dated three weeks before. The writing was spidery, but she recognized it as Cassie's and settled back to read:

Dearest Willow,
It was great seeing you the other day. I always enjoy your coming more than you'll ever know. I suppose they'll put a stop to it soon, though, because I'm getting weaker all the time. I hope to have this dollhouse done before long and am

rushing like crazy to finish it. You're probably wondering why I'm giving you another after all these years. I've never forgotten the one that was burned and how upset you were about its loss. I always meant to replace it, but somehow never got around to it. So I'm doing it now. I ordered the dollhouse kit from a company in the East, but I've made most of the furnishings myself.

I'm in a nostalgic mood tonight, and as I write this, so many memories of the wonderful times we've had together come to mind. Especially our trips to The Alamo, our picnics and the games we played there.

Willow stopped reading and smiled in fond remembrance of the outings she and Cassie used to enjoy to the original ranch house Addison's grandfather had built on the Clayton property a few miles from where the present house stood. The former ranch house had been abandoned for ages, and because of its Spanish style and the adobe wall that enclosed it, the girls had dubbed it The Alamo. Willow recalled how horrified Opal Andrews had been when she learned of their excursions to the place. She had forbidden them to go there, afraid that the ancient walls might topple down on them or that one of the girls would fall into the old dry well in the courtyard and break her neck. But they had disobeyed and spent many happy hours playing around the deserted ruins.

Willow hadn't thought of The Alamo for years, and she was filled with nostalgia when she looked back at Cassie's letter.

They're signaling lights out, so I'll finish this in the hope that I'll be seeing you again soon. Enjoy the dollhouse, and think of me whenever you look at it. And one more thing. Thank you for caring and for always being there for me. I've had numerous relationships in my life, as you know. So many, in fact, that if they were grains of sand, they'd probably fill a bucket. But none of them even come close to ours. We've had something very special, you and I, and I'll always be grateful for that.

A tight lump constricted Willow's throat as she put Cassie's letter back into the envelope.

Where to display the dollhouse?

She scanned the living room, but every nook and cranny was already filled to capacity. Then, recalling the tall maple hutch in the dining room, she carried the dollhouse in there. The hutch had a recessed space between the bottom cupboard, which held Willow's good china, then the glass-encased top shelves, which contained the heirloom crystal she'd inherited from her grandmother. The dollhouse fitted snugly into this niche.

Willow stepped back to admire the pretty little Victorian building before retrieving Cassie's letter, which she put in a drawer of the hutch. After burning the cardboard box in the fireplace, she turned her attention to Trixie. The dog had been padding in and out of the kitchen, giving broad hints that she wanted to be fed.

Willow didn't hear from Steven during the next few days, and wondered if he was settled into his condo and new job yet. Her own kept her so busy that she felt too tired at the end of one particularly hectic day to attend the aerobics class she occasionally attended. She decided to stay home instead.

After dinner Willow took a leisurely bath. As she emerged from the bathroom, she heard the wall phone in the kitchen ringing. It stopped shrilling before she could answer it, and she reasoned, mildly annoyed, that if the call was important, the caller would try again. She leafed through the TV section of the newspaper and, finding nothing that appealed to her, crawled into bed with a book of crossword puzzles, even though it was only seven-thirty. Trixie, seemingly content to make an early night of it, curled up in her basket a few feet away. Willow enjoyed working crossword puzzles, and in no time she became immersed in one.

A while later, however, when Trixie pawed at the rose-colored bedspread, Willow got up, stepped into her slippers and put a knee-length robe over her short nightgown. "Okay," she joked, following Trixie into the kitchen, "I'll let you out if you'll give me a nine-letter synonym for *obstruction*."

A blast of cold air rushed toward her when she opened the back door without bothering to snap on the porch light. She shivered from the piercing chill that snaked around her naked legs. Trixie dashed outside urgently, but skidded to an abrupt halt beside an evergreen tree in the middle of the yard. She sniffed the air, and her hackles stood erect.

A neighborhood cat sometimes strayed into the yard, and Trixie took fiendish delight in cornering it with a volley of vociferous barking. Thinking it was the cat Trixie scented, yet too tired to deal with the inevitable skirmish, Willow stepped outside to shoo the cat away.

Low-riding clouds hovered in a leaden sky devoid of moon and stars, as if they had been snatched away by a phantom hand seeking to cover the earth in darkness. The world seemed to be smothered in tomblike silence, and the pervasive gloom reminded her of the stygian blackness of an empty grave at midnight. A shiver rippled along Willow's spine. She rejected the morbid thought and glanced around the yard for the cat, her eyes squinting to peer through the inky blackness. As her searching gaze swept to the rear of the property, she spied the cat perched on the back fence, which divided Willow's yard from the one behind it. She moved quickly to prevent the cat from getting into the yard. At the same time the animal seemed to grow and change shape. Momentarily it became transformed into the head and shoulders of a shadowy human figure, which slithered over the fence.

Willow blinked, then came to a sudden stop beside Trixie. At first she thought the darkness was playing tricks with her eyes. But then the figure started stealthily toward her house, and an adrenaline rush of fear surged through her when she realized that it was real. The figure took another step, then another. Then, evidently as it spotted Willow and Trixie beside the tree, it froze.

Trixie's shrill barking shattered the silence as the dog bounded aggressively toward the frozen form. ''Trixie! No!'' Willow made a grab for Trixie, but she eluded her, and seized by sudden panic, Willow bolted for the house. Her heart thudding in her chest, she flew inside, slammed and locked the door. Then she sped to the phone to call the sheriff's office.

The disembodied male voice that answered her call assured her it would send someone out presently. Willow hung up, torn between relief and apprehension for Trixie. But her fear for herself intensified when she heard a loud thump somewhere near the back door.

Trixie had ceased barking all at once, and Willow wondered if the thump had been made by the dog wanting in. She listened for the sound of scratching on the door, but heavy silence prevailed. Her heart lurched when it came to her that the thumping noise had been made by the prowler rather than Trixie. Panic gripped Willow again as she wondered what to do if the prowler got in before the police arrived.

Despite her aversion to firearms, she regretted having vetoed the gun her father had wanted to buy her when she'd purchased the house and proposed to live there alone. It was too late to be thinking about that now. But at the unnerving thought, Willow grabbed a claw hammer from a nearby utility drawer. Then, deciding it would be poor protection at best, she rushed back to the telephone to call Eileen. As Willow dialed the number, she prayed that Eileen was home.

A groggy-sounding Eileen answered on the fifth ring, roused from sleep. Willow swiftly told her story, and Eileen said, her voice instantly alert, "Listen, honey, just sit tight; I'll send Mike right over."

In spite of the promise, Willow paced the floor in an agony of suspense. Where was Trixie? Why had the dog stopped barking so suddenly? Willow raced to the window and pressed her nose to the glass to see if she could find any sign of the dog or the shadowy figure. She discerned only dense darkness and started furiously when a harsh rasping sound erupted like a pistol shot in the hushed quiet.

She heaved a sigh of relief when she realized it was the sound of the side gate opening into the backyard. She surmised that Mike had opened the gate. Until then Willow had thought only of Trixie's safety and her own, but now she grew apprehensive for Mike's, as well. When his voice reached her through the kitchen door moments later she knew he was all right.

"Willow? It's me—Mike," he identified himself, and she hurried to let him in. Trixie followed, apparently unharmed, and Willow squatted to embrace her before turning back to Mike. He was armed with a fireplace poker and wore only a white T-shirt and tan cords. Setting the poker on the kitchen table, he explained, "When Eileen said you saw somebody messing around outside, I ran out in such a hurry, I forgot a jacket. I've checked things out, but didn't see anything. It probably wouldn't hurt to call the cops, anyway, though."

As if on cue, the doorbell rang. Willow went to let the police in. Mike trailed her, followed by Trixie.

Two deputies had responded to the call. Deputy Haggerty was stocky; Deputy Walters was thin. Willow led them into the living room, where Mike had already settled himself in the wing chair with Trixie at his feet, and described the scene in the backyard. They investigated the yard and returned to say that they had found no one.

Willow offered the deputies seats on either side of her on the sofa.

"Were you able to get a look at the intruder?" Haggerty asked. Walters was scribbling in a notepad he'd pulled from the pocket of his uniform.

"No. It was so dark I really couldn't see much of anything...." Willow paused as something suddenly occurred to her. "I *did* get an impression of dark clothing, now that I think of it," she continued. "In fact, whatever the person was wearing seemed to blend with the night."

"But you couldn't tell if it was a male or female?" Walters stopped writing to ask.

Willow had been so frightened that she hadn't given any thought to the gender of the shadowy figure. She did so now and shook her head. "I'm afraid not. I suppose it could have been either. But as I said, I really couldn't see all that well. Except for a domestic squabble a few weeks ago, this has always been a quiet neighborhood. I've never had any trouble. I hope tonight's episode isn't going to set a precedent," she said, voicing the thought that had been in her mind since she had telephoned the police. Willow shifted position to glance at Haggerty, who interjected a theory about the incident.

"I don't think there's anything to worry about. Did you know the house behind yours is an empty rental?" At Willow's nod, he went on. "We got a call last week from one of the neighbors complaining that the teenagers in the area are using the place for a love nest. It was probably one of them you saw cutting through your backyard. Too lazy to go around. You know how kids are. It looks like they're getting in through a broken window. We've contacted the owner to let him know what's going on, but we'll make sure he gets the window fixed. That should take care of the problem.''

Although Willow had known the house he spoke of was vacant, she hadn't been aware that it was being used as a trysting place. She felt enormously relieved.

Mike had sat by quietly while Willow talked to the two deputies, but now he said, ''I guess we got all shook up over nothing. I, for one, am sure glad to hear the neighborhood isn't going to the dogs. No reflection on you,'' he said to Trixie.

When the policemen stood to leave, Mike went into the kitchen for his poker. He carried it somewhat sheepishly now, embarrassed by the news that no threat had existed after all. In the entry hall, Willow thanked the officers and turned a grateful smile on Mike as he accompanied them out.

A few minutes later the telephone rang, and Willow hurried into the kitchen to answer it.

''I didn't come over because I've got rollers in my hair and didn't want anybody to see me,'' Eileen said without preamble. Willow grinned, recalling that rollers in her hair hadn't stopped Eileen from appearing on the scene when the couple who lived on the other side of her broke into a loud screaming match in their front yard late at night. ''Mike says the cops think it was some kid you saw in your backyard. Is that right?''

Willow agreed that it was, and Eileen observed, her tone benign, ''Typical kids. But just the same, it must've scared the heck out of you. Are you still nervous? Want me to come and keep you company for a while?''

Although Willow owned that she'd been shaken, she was fine now. She thanked Eileen but declined her offer.

Willow climbed back into bed to finish the crossword puzzle she'd been working. She found it difficult to regain her former interest in the puzzle.

Half an hour later she was interrupted once more by the chiming of the doorbell. Wondering if the police had perhaps returned, Willow got up and got on her robe and slippers again. Since it was after nine, she looked cautiously through the peephole before opening the door.

Steven Randall stood captured in the golden arc of the porch light. Willow let him in and said, her voice mirroring her surprise, "I was thinking about you the other day. I wondered if you'd gotten settled in your new place and job." He took the wing chair Mike had vacated earlier, Willow the cushioned rocker a few feet away. But even from this distance she was aware of the way his vital presence dominated the room.

"Yes to both. I just came from a café I've adopted near the courthouse and decided to drop by instead of phoning to ask you to dinner tomorrow night."

Steven lit a cigarette and leaned back in his chair. Although she still had misgivings about going out with him, she'd already agreed to do so and couldn't think of a legitimate excuse to turn him down. She was about to say yes when she noticed something about him that she hadn't been aware of until then.

He was dressed in jeans, a dark blue shirt, navy parka and black boots. As he stretched his long legs out in front of him, Willow saw the trace of dampness that darkened the hem of his jeans. The image of the shadowy figure she'd seen outside flashed into her mind. Whereas it had only been a faceless outline before, now it assumed definite features—those of Steven.

Dark clothing. Wetness around the hem of his pants. A coincidence? Or something more?

In the next instant Willow recalled the incident at the ranch. She'd thought of Steven initially, then ultimately blamed it on an overzealous newspaper reporter. Could the intruder in her room really have been Steven—and again tonight? The deputy had conjectured that a teenager had cut through her backyard. Maybe his theory was wrong. Though Willow couldn't fathom why Steven would rifle through her belongings or skulk around her house at night, the possibility that he had done so gave her a creepy feeling.

Steven took another drag of his cigarette as he waited for Willow's reply. She'd agreed to have dinner with him, so he was confident she wouldn't back out now, but she certainly seemed to be taking her sweet time about it. He glanced at her, noticing how different she looked from when he'd seen her last.

Willow had been the chic career woman when Steven had lunched with her. Now, with her tousled midnight hair tumbling down around her shoulders, she looked like a guileless virgin unaware of her own sexual allure. Her knee-length robe displayed legs that were slender, shapely, with fine-boned ankles. They had the delicate quality of a Thoroughbred racehorse. He didn't think the lady would appreciate that comparison. Besides, Willow was taking so long to answer that in spite of his confidence he was beginning to wonder if she intended to back out after all.

Steven looked at her face and saw that she was staring at him. Her gray eyes were intent, speculative, suspicious. "Is something wrong?" he asked.

"I'm not sure...." Willow hesitated, wondering if she should tell him what was on her mind, then deciding to tell him and study his reaction. "I caught a prowler in my backyard a while ago, and the police left not long before you came. I—"

"Is everything okay? You're not hurt or anything, are you?" Steven broke in, concern etched in his face.

"I'm fine. But I'm positive whoever it was was wearing something dark...." She let her voice trail away, her pointed glance move slowly over his clothing.

"Surely you aren't implying it was me?" Steven's voice was full of shocked incredulity. His eyes grew cool all at once, and his features took on the appearance of granite. He leaned forward, his look interrogating Willow from across the room.

"I have to admit I *am* wondering." Her own gaze was challenging, and she refused to allow his obvious indignation to dissuade her. "This isn't the first time something's happened, either. Somebody searched my suitcase the night before Cassie's memorial service. And—"

"I was at the ranch," Steven cut in once more, "so you think it was me. Is that right?" The glacial anger in his face was almost frightening, but Willow refused to let that intimidate her. "Well, it wasn't," he said vehemently. "What reason would I have for going through your suitcase? And why the hell would I be prowling around here, anyway?"

"I have no idea. I thought maybe *you* could tell me," Willow countered. Steven's anger was contagious. She was becoming irritated herself and she didn't care if he knew it.

He did know it, and decided he'd better do something or he would lose the ball game in the first inning. His voice became persuasive, deliberately gentle. "Look, I can see that in your eyes the evidence is pretty well stacked against me. But I swear it wasn't me either time. I told you the truth when I said I'd just finished eating before I got here."

Willow remembered having read somewhere that a person's eyebrows quirked when he or she was telling a lie. She looked closely at Steven's, but they remained fixed in place. His expression was so pleading, so seemingly sincere, that she wondered if he might actually be as innocent as he claimed.

She realized that her thoughts must have shown in her face when Steven said, "Am I right in thinking you believe me?" Willow opened her mouth to say that she honestly didn't know. But before she could speak he reminded her, "You still haven't said if you'll have dinner with me tomorrow night. Are we on?"

"I guess so," Willow said, conscious of the uncertainty in her tone. She was aware as well of the wide grin Steven gave her, which ebbed and flowed around her like a warm tide.

Steven didn't have to feign his pleased smile. He was both pleased and monumentally relieved, because he knew that if Willow chose to make herself inaccessible, he would have had to devise another way of reaching his primary objective. That would have complicated the situation severely. "I'll pick you up at

seven. We can decide then where we want to eat.''
With that, he stood up, said good-night and hurriedly
strode out, as if, Willow mused, closing the door behind him, he were afraid she might change her mind.

As she padded into her bedroom once more, it occurred to her that despite Steven's declaration of innocence, she really had no way of knowing whether he
was innocent. She considered the matter at length. In
the end, she decided to set aside her suspicions and
take him at his word.

Unless, of course, something else happened to rouse
them again.

Chapter Four

The various aspects of her job kept Willow so busy the next day that it wasn't until she returned home at five-thirty that she was able to turn her thoughts to the evening ahead.

She found the prospect of spending it in Steven's company a pleasant one, and her pride demanded that she look her best. She opened her bedroom closet door and cast a critical eye over her wardrobe. Her choice was a dress of emerald-green crepe de chine with a draped neckline, which dipped low enough to reveal just the right amount of cleavage.

The doorbell chimed promptly at seven, and she summoned a smile as she let Steven in. He presented a striking picture as he stood framed in the doorway. He was wearing a gray wool suit with a burgundy silk tie. The expert tailoring of his dark gray overcoat accented his powerful shoulders, and his white shirt deepened his tan. Willow was glad she'd chosen the green dress. Anything less becoming would have made her feel dowdy.

Steven returned her greeting, betraying his awareness of her appreciative glance only by the amused tilt of his mouth. "It's cold enough out there to freeze a polar bear's teeth. You'd better wear a warm wrap," he advised her, closing the door.

"Thanks for the warning. I'll keep that in mind." Willow noted the way Steven's eyes roamed over her with candid approval. She had wondered if he was the kind of man to compliment a woman on her appearance, and even though he said nothing, his frank appreciation flattered her no less than words. She experienced a surge of feminine satisfaction as she turned to lead him into the living room.

Steven followed, his glance sliding along Willow's back before it dropped to her narrow waist. He observed the gentle sway of her hips and how the soft fabric of her dress molded her slender buttocks and thighs. The heels of her black patent leather pumps were extremely high, yet she carried herself with the proud posture of a ballerina.

"I trust you were all right after I left last night. I . . . er . . . that is, I hope nothing else happened. . . ." Steven's voice trailed away, a dark flush creeping over his face, and he shifted position as if uncomfortable.

Willow wondered if he realized that his first statement could be taken two ways, either as a polite inquiry or as an admission of guilt. However, if he was responsible for the previous evening's incident, he surely wouldn't be stupid enough to have made such a blunder. Or would he? In spite of having decided to give him the benefit of the doubt, she was torn by uncertainty again. She gave him a quizzical look before replying.

"Yes, I was all right. And no, nothing else happened."

Steven was keenly aware of that questing gaze, of the indecisive light in Willow's eyes. He inwardly cursed his inarticulate tongue for its clumsiness. The last thing he wanted was to rekindle her suspicion of him. He had intended to avoid the episode entirely, but had subsequently decided that not mentioning it might seem odd. To get Willow's mind on something else, he schooled his features to bland innocence. "Have you thought about where you'd like to eat?"

To Steven's intense relief, her doubtful expression subsided. It was replaced by a slow smile that quirked the corners of her beautifully sculptured mouth. "Well, actually, I thought we could decide that together."

Having discovered from past experience how fragile the male ego was, Willow was reluctant to admit she'd been so busy during the day that she hadn't had time to think about their date, let alone where she wanted to go. She added diplomatically, "We could look in the entertainment section of the newspaper, if you like."

"I don't think that's necessary. I asked around today for a good place to eat, and somebody recommended Steamboat Landing. I took the liberty of making a reservation there. I hope that's okay with you?"

It was, and Willow said as much. Steamboat Landing was an authentic 1850s riverboat that had been converted into a restaurant-inn-theater. The place was reportedly high priced, and she was impressed with Steven's willingness to take her there.

Cottony clouds formed a thick canopy overhead when they stepped outside a few minutes later. The temperature had taken a dramatic plunge since Willow had walked home from the courthouse; the air held the promise of snow. She burrowed deeper into her white, waist-length rabbit-fur coat to ward off the chill, which seemed to seep into her bones.

Steven led her to a classic black Jaguar that stood at the curb in front of the house. As he opened Willow's door, then strode around to the driver's side, she admired the fancy grillwork on the hood, the tufted leather on the seats and dashboard. Real estate was indeed a lucrative enterprise. Either that, or Steven had income from another source. The sudden thought sparked Willow's curiosity. When Steven slid behind the wheel, she commented, "If selling real estate means I can drive a car like this, I'm quitting my job tomorrow morning. Think you could get me on where you work?"

Steven chuckled, but withheld his response until he had eased the Jaguar out into the street. "I'd be glad to, only I don't think they're hiring right now. Besides, I doubt my annual income from real estate is much more than yours."

"Then . . . ?"

Willow stopped herself, afraid Steven might think she was being nosy. He must have known what she was going to say, because he explained, "My folks are in the hotel business in Arizona. I'm a silent partner, much to my father's disappointment. I don't think he's ever really forgiven me for not following family tradition as he did when he inherited the chain." Steven laughed, but ruefully.

"Yet you didn't. Follow family tradition, I mean."
She peered through the windshield as they sped along
the highway toward the outskirts of town.

"No. I chose to go in another direction," Steven
remarked, without going into his reasons for having
done so. Not wishing to seem too inquisitive, Willow
didn't press the issue. Soon after, he swung the Jaguar into the parking lot of Steamboat Landing and
turned it over to an attendant before coming around
to open Willow's door.

Moored in concrete, the triple-decked paddle-
wheeler boasted white wooden filigree work around its
railings and decks. His hand on her elbow, Steven led
her up a wide gangplank to the lower deck where a
reservation desk had been placed.

The maître d' seated them at a table for two. A
cocktail waitress brought their drinks—a piña colada
for Willow, a gin and tonic for Steven.

Steven took a sip of his gin and said, his glance
sweeping over the Corinthian columns that ran the
length of the room, "Not bad, huh?"

"Not bad at all." Willow's gaze lifted to the elaborate Gothic arches that decorated the ceiling.

"This sort of reminds me of the architecture you see
in Europe," Steven observed. "Ever been there?"

"No, but I'd like to someday. I take it you have."

"I knocked around the Continent for a while after
I got out of college." Steven went on to mention some
of the cities he'd visited, and Willow listened with
genuine interest while they finished their cocktails.

When a waiter brought them menus, she noted the
absence of a price list and wondered wryly what would
happen if an imprudent diner hadn't brought enough

money to pay the check. But Steven evidently wasn't worried about that.

"According to the guy who recommended this place, the lobster tail's outstanding. Shall we give it a try?"

"Umm, by all means." The entrée tasted as delectable as it sounded, and Willow enjoyed it until they reached the halfway point in the meal.

In spite of the waiter's having loosened the lobster, a small section still adhered stubbornly to the shell, so she gave it a gentle nudge with her fork to pry it away. When that failed to dislodge it, she tried again, this time with more force. Willow watched with horrified fascination as the piece of lobster flipped across the table to land just inside the breast pocket of Steven's suit. It perched there ludicrously, looking for all the world like an anemic, misshapen basketball trapped in the rim of the net.

Steven stared down at it with stunned astonishment.

When Willow was finally able to speak, her voice came out in an agonized groan. "Oh, God . . . Steven, I'm so sorry. Really, I... It was stuck in the shell, and I..."

She came to a stumbling halt, the heat of humiliation stinging her cheeks. She'd always prided herself on having some degree of sophistication, but at that moment she felt gauche, inexperienced, like a country bumpkin unused to city ways. She wished the floor would open up and swallow her. Unable to stand the intense quiet from Steven's side of the table, she stole a glance at him through her lashes, mentally bracing herself for the annoyance she felt certain she would encounter.

Steven's features became wreathed with amusement. He plucked the offensive morsel of shellfish from his pocket and set it on the edge of his plate, then burst into laughter. "I'll bet you were great at tiddly-winks when you were a kid," he teased. The unsightly smear of melted butter that ruined his suit coat made her flush crimson again.

Steven dunked the end of his napkin into his water goblet and dabbed ineffectively at the stain. Willow had lapsed into embarrassed silence again, and the acute distress on her face stifled his amusement and moved him to unexpected sympathy. "It's no big deal," he reassured her. "The suit can be cleaned, you know. Now let's forget about it and finish our dinner."

Forgetting wasn't that easy for Willow. Steven guessed as much and prompted further, "I've told you about my travels in Europe, but I haven't given you a chance to say anything about yourself—what you like to do, for instance."

Willow replied gratefully, "Well, I like gardening, dancing, doing crossword puzzles and reading a good book." Listed so flatly, her leisure activities sounded quite boring. She added with a rueful smile, "Pretty dull, huh? Maybe I should take up white-water rafting or cliff diving to put some excitement in my life."

"I've tried 'em. They *are* exciting. But sometimes I enjoy doing more placid things, like working with wood and painting. I'm afraid I'm only a dabbler, though," Steven admitted with a deprecatory grin. "Cassie had quite a flair for painting, as I recall. I saw a seascape and a pastoral scene she did, and I was really impressed. It's a damned shame, her pulling that robbery and ending up dying in prison...such a waste of her talent. Especially when she didn't need the money. And even if she had needed it, it wouldn't have done her any good behind bars.''

''No, it wouldn't have,'' Willow agreed. ''But you're right about Cassie's being talented. She was one of those rare people who did well at almost anything she tried. I always envied her for that.'' She sighed. Then, remembering the Victorian dollhouse, added on a brighter note, ''Speaking of Cassie's cleverness, you should see the dollhouse she sent me the other day. She made almost all the furniture herself and did a wonderful job. It's a real gem.''

Having finished eating, Steven lit a cigarette and gazed at Willow through a blue haze of smoke. ''Oh? You mean her family gave it to you as a remembrance of Cassie?''

''No, it came from Cassie herself. Well, actually, it was sent to me from the prison by one of the guards. Cassie had evidently been working on it before she got sick.''

Willow went on to describe the miniature Victorian. When she paused in her narrative, Steven remarked, ''You've obviously gotten attached to it already. But aren't you kind of big to be playing with toys? I thought dollhouses were supposed to be for little girls.'' His tone was light, bantering, but the way his brown eyes strayed downward to linger on the swell of Willow's breasts implied that she was definitely a full-grown woman and a very appealing one at that.

She ignored the tingle of awareness his clinging gaze produced and explained that Cassie had given her the dollhouse to replace the original one. "Besides, Mr. Smart Guy, they aren't necessarily considered toys. A lot of adults collect them today, and they were popular with royalty at one time. Queen Victoria even had one and commissioned the best craftsmen to design and furnish it for her. Remind me to show you mine when you take me home. You'll see what I mean about Cassie's cleverness."

After dessert and espresso, the two watched an entertaining version of Agatha Christie's *The Mousetrap*. It was snowing lightly when they left the riverboat a while later. Steven was quiet as he skillfully guided the Jaguar through the unplowed streets. Willow relaxed against the seat, and neither of them spoke until they had reached her house.

"Brr. This is a good night for a hot buttered rum. Or would you rather have a brandy instead?" Willow acknowledged Trixie's greeting and switched off the television while Steven shed his overcoat.

Although Willow had managed to overcome the mortification of her accident, his suit coat bore mute testimony to it now. When he opted for hot buttered rum, she suggested, "Come into the kitchen with me. I've got some spot remover that should take care of that awful stain." Steven looked as if he might protest, and she hurried into the kitchen, leaving him with no choice but to follow.

While Willow took out the cleaning fluid and a cloth, Steven started to shrug out of the jacket. She stopped him. "I think I can do it while you've got it on. The spot remover shouldn't go through and wet your shirt.'' To make sure it didn't, she used her left hand as a protective shield between his coat and shirt.

Her palm rested lightly on Steven's chest. Dabbing at the greasy smear, she could feel the solid mass of muscles, the warmth that emanated from him, his breath on her temples. His heart beat a steady tattoo beneath her hand, and at this close proximity she saw a tiny nick in his chin. The bronzed column of his throat looked smooth but strong, and she wondered if it would feel as smooth to the touch as it appeared. She had a sudden urge to run exploratory fingers along the side of his neck, but resisted it.

Steven suffered Willow's ministrations, his expression one of amused indulgence. He couldn't have cared less about the suit and had given in only to humor her. Although he'd known she was small, he hadn't noticed until then how petite she really was; the top of her head barely reached his shoulders. The light caught her hair and turned it to black satin. The fresh clean scent of it drifted to him, redolent of flowers, and involuntarily he leaned forward, first to sniff the silky tresses, then to take a swath between his fingers. It felt like velvet.

He sniffed her hair again, then released the dark strands. "Hmm. Nice. Gardenia?"

"Jasmine. It's my shampoo." Willow was pleased by the compliment, yet very much aware of Steven's nearness. Her efforts completed, she stepped back with a smile. "There you go. You won't smell so hot until it dries." She wrinkled her pert nose at the pungent odor, then cautioned him, "And whatever you do, don't light a cigarette until it does. That stuff's inflammable."

"Don't worry, I won't. But how about showing me the dollhouse Cassie gave you. After the way you extolled its virtues, I'm curious to see it."

"Oh, sure. You see it while I fix our drinks. It's right through there." Willow pointed him toward the dining room before assembling the ingredients for the hot buttered rum. She called to him when it was ready a few minutes later, but got no response, so she went into the dining room to call him again.

She found him standing in front of the maple hutch. His body was hunched over as he peered into the little Victorian structure through the double doors at the rear, which he had opened. He had turned the dollhouse sideways as well, to give himself a better look inside. Though his profile was turned toward her, he didn't seem to notice her, and she watched unobserved while he studied all three floors.

Steven's obvious interest in the miniature both surprised and pleased Willow. He must have been impressed by Cassie's craftsmanship or he wouldn't have admired the dollhouse for so long. "I told you it was a gem, didn't I?" she remarked with a knowing grin.

"Yes, and you were right. Cassie really outdid herself. The fire in the hearth of the parlor looks like it's actually burning." Steven straightened, closed the doors and turned the dollhouse back to its right position. "Now, what about that drink?"

As they sipped the hot rum, they discussed the meal, which Willow conceded had been excellent. "I hear their barbecued spareribs are supposed to be pretty good, too. Maybe we should give them a try sometime."

Steven was tempted to add that he'd be sure to wear a goalie's outfit in case she got dangerous with the ribs, but he was afraid a joke might antagonize her, and that was something he couldn't afford to do. Instead, he put his mug down on the coffee table to pet Trixie, who'd parked herself at his feet.

Willow had put on a cassette tape of The Moody Blues that contained all their older hits. She'd had it since she was a teenager, but it was still one of her favorites. Evidently it was a favorite of Steven's, too, because he said, "That has some great songs on it, doesn't it? I've got that tape, too. Are they still together?"

"Last I heard they were, but I think they've changed their sound a little. Since you like The Moody Blues, does that mean your taste in music runs to soft rock?" She glanced at his jacket, relieved to see that no trace remained of the smear.

Steven saw where she was looking and grinned. "I have to admit that really did the trick. Actually, I like everything from Pavarotti to Willie Nelson, and a lot in between."

In the course of the conversation they discovered they had similar tastes in music. Steven refused another drink.

"Thanks, but I'd better be going. It's getting late."

The digital clock on the VCR said it was after ten. As Steven rose and picked up his overcoat, Willow thanked him for the dinner and play.

"I'm glad you liked them. I'll have to tell the guy who recommended the place that he was right on."

After Steven had driven away, Willow collected their mugs, carried them into the kitchen and loaded the dishwasher. It occurred to her that, except for Steven's remark about his income, he hadn't talked about his job all evening. Most of the men she had dated talked about their jobs all the time. The attorney with whom she'd been involved had discussed business so much that she'd grown bored with hearing about deeds, wills, assigns and such.

Since Steven had so recently begun his current job, she would have thought he'd at least have said something about how he was coping with it. Perhaps he had avoided the subject because he'd thought she wouldn't be interested. But still, the omission was unusual.

Chapter Five

The next day turned out to be hectic. Willow spent it bouncing back and forth between juvenile, criminal and civil courts with no time to catch her breath after each session. By the end of the afternoon she was so tired, her nerves so frayed, that she wanted nothing more than to sit back and relax. But there was a week's grocery shopping to do, so she got into her Camaro and drove to the market at the north end of town.

The weather had warmed, and it had begun to drizzle lightly as she left the courthouse. By the time she'd finished shopping and started home, it was raining so hard that she had to slow the Camaro to a crawl and squint to see through the streaming windshield. It was tedious, nerve-racking. As if the rain wasn't enough to contend with, however, the steering wheel gave a sudden lurch, and a rough thumping signaled a flat tire.

"Oh, fantastic! That's all I need!" With a muttered curse, Willow eased the car off the road and killed the engine. Then, to curb her irritation, she bent her head against the steering wheel and counted to twenty. Her father had taught her to change a tire when he had bought her first car, so she was fully capable of fixing a flat. She simply didn't relish having to do it in the torrential downpour. She decided to wait, hoping the rain would slacken.

When several minutes later it hadn't, she jerked the keys from the ignition, got out and promptly stepped into a slushy mud puddle in the new leather boots she was wearing for the first time. She had forgotten until then that she had them on. With an annoyed "Damn!" she ducked her uncovered head and groped her way through the rain-swept darkness to the trunk.

Collecting the spare, jack and lug wrench, she squatted down and was just about to begin the irksome task of changing the flat when she saw a flash of headlights from a vehicle that had just come to a stop behind hers.

Willow straightened and peered through the wet tendrils of hair plastered to her face at the approaching figure of a man wearing a raincoat and a broad-brimmed hat pulled down over his eyes. She couldn't make out any detail of his features. She smiled gratefully, but her smile faded abruptly when she recalled the recent trial of a rapist who preyed on lone women with car trouble.

Gratitude fled, to be replaced by uneasiness when a glance around showed her that there wasn't another vehicle in sight. Willow wished she'd taken a class in self-defense or carried a can of mace in her purse and wondered apprehensively what to do. She had no intention of becoming his victim if she could help it. She looked around for something she could use as protection, and spying the lug wrench, snatched it up. Her body braced for a fight, her heart palpitating, she watched the man approach. His head was lowered, his stride purposeful.

"Willow?" he called, and relief spread through her when she recognized his voice.

"Oh, Mike, thank heaven it's you." Willow released a gusty sigh as he came to a halt beside her. "For a minute I thought—"

"I think I can imagine what you thought," Mike broke in, obviously amused. "What were you going to do, brain me with that thing?" He nodded down at the lug wrench, which she was holding at the ready.

"Something like that," Willow admitted with a sheepish grin. "With that rain gear on, I couldn't tell it was you."

"Well, I'm glad you don't pack a pistol. You might have gotten nervous and picked me off before I could say anything."

Mike explained that he was on his way back from Reno. He had spotted her car at the side of the road and stopped to see if she had run out of gas. Now he insisted on changing the flat tire while Willow waited in the car. Afterward, he followed her home to make sure she got there without any more mishaps. When Mike swung into Eileen's driveway, Willow tooted her horn to thank him yet again. By the time she had carried in the groceries, she looked like a drowned duck. Her boots were badly stained with mud, and her beige coat was soaked and mud-streaked, as well.

Willow had just finished cleaning herself up when Eileen knocked on the door.

"It's a nasty night, huh? I could swear I saw Noah's Ark float past on my way over." Eileen closed her umbrella and shook it, sprinkling the entry hall with raindrops. "Mike told me he did his good deed for the day by changing your tire. He's a regular little Boy Scout, isn't he?" As always, her voice softened at the mention of Mike's name.

"Not a Boy Scout, a Good Samaritan. Or a knight on a white charger. Even if, in this case, the white charger was a green Toyota."

"Right. He said you nearly attacked him with a lug wrench."

Willow conceded that she had, and they both laughed. Willow was feeling a bit foolish now that her scare was over.

"I came over to see if I could borrow your crystal candlesticks," Eileen explained. "We're having Mike's boss and his wife for dinner tonight, and Mike wants to make a good impression."

"Sure. They're in the dining room. I'll get them for you."

Eileen trailed after her and exclaimed, "Oh, how pretty! When did you get this?" She was eyeing the dollhouse with admiration.

"Just a few days ago. It was sent from the prison where Cassie was."

"You mean they let her take it to jail with her?"

"No. From what she said in the letter that came with the dollhouse, she ordered the kit while she was there. She made most of the stuff inside herself." Willow's fingers fondly traced the white picket fence that enclosed the front of the dollhouse. She explained why Cassie had given it to her. "I'd almost forgotten about the other one, but, bless her, Cassie hadn't."

Willow turned the little Victorian structure sideways and opened the rear panels so that Eileen could see inside.

"Boy, she did a great job. Oh—look at this." Eileen took a tiny rattle from the cradle in the nursery, gave it a shake and laughed when it emitted a soft clattering sound. She explored the four rooms with delight while Willow got down the candlesticks.

In the entry hall on her way out, Eileen asked, "By the way, have you had any more trouble with kids cutting through your backyard?"

"Fortunately, no. Only I'm not so sure now it was teenagers."

Eileen had stooped for her umbrella but now turned to Willow with a quizzical look. "What do you mean? You think it was somebody else?"

"I don't know and I really have no proof. But there's this guy I met at the Clayton ranch the day Cassie died, and he showed up not long after the police left the other night. He was wearing dark clothes, like whoever I saw. I guess it *could* have been a coincidence. But..." Feeling a sudden need to confide her doubts about Steven, Willow decided to tell Eileen about her suitcase having been searched at the ranch. Eileen spoke before she could do so.

"Wait a minute. You mean you've got a new man in your life, and this is the first I've heard of it?" Eileen's expression was curious and a little hurt at the same time.

"I didn't say anything because there really wasn't anything to tell. I didn't even know I'd be seeing him. I still don't," Willow explained, remembering that except for tentatively mentioning the possibility of taking her back to Steamboat Landing, Steven had said nothing about whether he intended to ask her out again.

"You think he could be a Peeping Tom or a weirdo who gets his kicks by peeking in women's windows?" Eileen asked, her hazel eyes filled with concern.

Willow considered the question and shook her head. Despite her misgivings about Steven, he didn't strike her as the type to resort to voyeurism. "I'd say women would be more apt to be peeking through his windows. He's very attractive." A sudden loud clap of thunder accompanied her words. The wind had risen, too, and she could hear it howling through the eaves of the house. It sounded like a thousand lost souls shrieking in torment and gave her a slightly eerie feeling. Eileen did nothing to allay it.

"Well, for heaven's sake, be careful, honey. This may be a small town, but I'm sure it has its share of kooks. You don't know what's out there."

To illustrate her point, Eileen told Willow about a teacher she'd once known who had been engaged to a man for six months before she learned he was an escaped homicidal maniac. "The sicko hacked his grandmother up, then buried her all over the yard. I guess it took the police a while to find all of the poor thing."

On that grisly note she left. As Willow bolted the door behind her and traipsed back into the kitchen, she couldn't shake her feeling of unease. She realized that she was being silly; there couldn't possibly be that many homicidal maniacs running around loose. And even if there were, Steven surely had no such tendencies. Still, after Eileen's horror story, Willow found it difficult to relax for some time.

ALTHOUGH WILLOW FAILED to hear from Steven, she received a visit from an unexpected source. As she left her office a couple of days later on her way home, she met Brad Clayton in the downstairs corridor of the courthouse.

"Well, hi, Brad. What in the world are you doing here?" Willow's friendly smile was tinged with surprise when he came to stand beside her. They were blocking the path of people emerging from the courtroom, and Brad led her to a bench set against the wall.

"I'm in town on business and I decided to drop by to see how you were. Actually, I was thinking maybe we could have a drink together. I've been stuck in a meeting for hours with nothing but men, so I could use some feminine company right now—especially if that feminine company happens to be attractive."

The admiring look that accompanied his remark told Willow that she very much fitted into that category. She was woman enough to feel complimented by it. But Brad's invitation made her curious, too. Though he'd always been pleasant, he had never shown the least sign of interest in her. If anything, he'd treated her with the same casual indifference he displayed toward his sisters when they were growing up. She wondered what made him realize suddenly that she was an unrelated female. Also, her intuition told her that there was more to Brad's having looked her up than the simple desire to find out how she was.

Inquisitive about this as well, Willow went with him to a cocktail lounge. There she discovered that her instincts had been right.

As they sipped their drinks in a quiet corner, Brad gave her a boyish smile. "I'm glad you came. Not only for your company, but...well...there's something I wanted to talk to you about. I realize you've told the family about your last visit with Cassie. It must have been a traumatic experience, being with her when she died. But I've been wondering if, now that you've had time to get over it, you've thought of anything you might have forgotten to mention when you were at the ranch."

"Like what?" Willow gave him an inquiring look over the small disk of the table.

"Well, I was hoping you'd remembered something Cassie said to indicate where the two million dollars from the armored-car robbery could be. Look, Willow," Brad rushed on before she could frame a reply, "I really hate to nag you. But you can't imagine the hell the family's been through since this thing happened. The Clayton name's always been an honorable one, but even now, after all these months, some people are treating us like we had something to do with the robbery. I guess you know Dad's political opponents have milked it for all it's worth. I don't think it'll end until the money's been found, if it ever is. So we'd appreciate anything you can do to help the situation."

Whereas Addison's attitude when he'd questioned Willow about the money had been ruthlessly determined, Brad's was hopeful, pleading. Despite the fact that she knew he had approached her only for possible information, she somehow couldn't be annoyed with him. She wondered if Brad had sought her out on his own or if Addison had put him up to it. She suspected the latter and had no doubt that if she were able to shed any light on the disappearance of the money, Addison would try to find a way to take credit for its recovery. For what better way to impress the public and his political constituents than by solving the mystery of the missing two million dollars himself?

Willow had already told Addison she knew nothing about it and repeated that now to Brad. "You could have saved yourself the price of a drink and called me instead," she added wryly.

"That wasn't the only reason I wanted to see you again," Brad quickly assured her. "You know, it's funny, but until you came to the ranch to bring Cassie's letter, I'd always thought of you as a kid. But I realized then what an attractive woman you've become."

He reached across the table to cover Willow's hands with his. She felt flattered by his interest and returned the warm pressure of his fingers, yet she was practical enough to ask, "What about your wife? Cassie said you and she were separated. Is there any chance of a reconciliation?"

"I doubt it. Too many problems...." Brad lapsed into silence as if contemplating those problems. Then he returned to the original subject. "So you can't think of anything further to add?"

"No. I'm sorry. Cassie never discussed the robbery or the money. So she couldn't have said anything to me about where it was. Besides, the guy who was caught with her was the only one who ever said she knew where it was. Frankly, I think he lied, hoping to get a lighter sentence."

"Maybe. But I felt I had to ask, just the same." Brad released Willow's hands to toss back the last of his whiskey and soda. The expression on his face showed such disappointment that she searched for a way to brighten his mood. The topic of Cassie quite naturally brought to mind the miniature Victorian house, so she told him about that.

"She got you a dollhouse for your birthday or something a long time ago, didn't she? I remember she showed it to me and was all excited about giving it to you, because it was what you really wanted the most. Why did she get you another one after all these years?" Brad still looked disappointed, and Willow guessed he was brooding about the money.

She started to tell him the reason, but he signaled the cocktail waitress for another drink, so she finished her white wine instead. The second round arrived, and by then she had remembered something else. "Did you know Steven Randall has moved here?"

"No. And I didn't know where he lived, anyway."

"Reno. But I thought you already knew that, since you were the one who introduced him to me. I guess I just automatically assumed you and Steven were friends."

"You assumed wrong. I never laid eyes on him till the day Cassie died, and he showed up at the ranch. Randall said he was her friend and that he had come to pay his respects to the family. I gather you've seen him again."

"Two or three times. I thought he was Cassie's friend, too. But I don't remember her ever mentioning him. Do you?'' Willow had picked up her glass, but set it down again, surprised by Brad's information.

''No. I'm sure she never said anything to me about him. I thought about it when he was at the ranch. Apparently she never did to Dad or Jennifer, either. I asked them. What does this Randall do for a living, anyway?'' The abstracted look had left Brad's eyes and interest gleamed in their blue depths.

''He says he's in real estate, only he doesn't talk about it. At least he didn't when I had dinner with him the other night.'' Brad's series of negatives had brought a puzzled frown to Willow's smooth brow.

''Well, maybe he dislikes what he's doing, so he doesn't talk about it. Or maybe being with a pretty lady like you made him forget business. It certainly would me.'' Brad's admiring gaze reached out to encompass Willow, but she was too bewildered at the moment to appreciate it. ''Or there could be another reason,'' he continued. ''He could be handing you a line. Some guys enjoy playing games. Personally, that kind of thing's always seemed immature and unnecessary to me. But...'' Brad shrugged, perplexed by the foibles of his own sex.

''You mean you think he could be lying? Why on earth would he do that?'' Willow knew that her questions were just an echo of what she'd been thinking all along.

''Maybe he has a mediocre job and thought being in real estate sounded more sophisticated. Who knows? You know the guy better than I do,'' Brad countered. A group of businessmen at another table broke into guffaws, as though one of them had made a risqué remark. Brad's glance slid momentarily to them before returning to Willow. "Besides, it was only a suggestion. I have to admit I wondered about Randall myself, but now you've really made me curious."

Join the club! Willow thought sardonically, although curiosity was mild in comparison to what she was feeling. Willow's instincts had told her there was more to Steven Randall than appeared on the surface, and now Brad had told her that he had dropped from out of the blue, declaring himself Cassie's friend, when those closest to her had never heard of him. That Steven was an unknown quantity was glaringly apparent. But who was he? More important, *what* was he?

The questions reduced Willow to silence. Absorbed in his own reflections, Brad was quiet, as well.

That evening, when Willow went about her nightly routine, her movements were mechanical, her mind detached from the tasks she performed, her thoughts filled with the enigma that was Steven Randall.

Chapter Six

Now that Brad had suggested that Steven didn't discuss his job because it simply didn't exist, Willow was
inquisitive enough to find out. She recalled his having
said he was employed at Nationwide Realty Company and decided to give the place a call the first
chance she got.

The opportunity came the next day during her midmorning break. She dialed the first few digits, only to
hesitate on the last one. Checking up on Steven this
way made her feel devious, sneaky, the reverse of the
up-front person she'd always considered herself. But
dammit, there were just too many unexplained factors involved, too many peculiarities about him for
comfort. The reminder banished Willow's reserva-
tions, and with a determined look, she completed the
call.

When a cheerful feminine voice announced that she
had reached the correct number, Willow asked for
Steven.

"Steven Randall? I don't think he's in right now,
but let me put you on hold a minute to make sure." A
click in Willow's ear was followed by the sound of

dead air, which lasted an unreasonable length of time. The woman's minute turned out to be more like five. Thinking that she'd forgotten she had put her on hold, Willow was about to hang up and dial the number again when she came back on the line.

"Sorry to keep you waiting so long. Somebody came in asking for directions. Steven is out of the office right now. May I take a message or have him return your call?"

"I . . . uh . . . no, thank you. I'll try again later." Although she knew she should have anticipated the question, it flustered Willow and she stumbled over her reply. As she severed the connection, she gave an absent smile to a bailiff who was striding past her open office door. So Steven was precisely what he claimed to be, at least where his job was concerned. There were a couple of things that still troubled her about him, of course, but the knowledge that Steven hadn't lied after all made her feel better just the same.

When her break was over, Willow returned to the courtroom. As always, she concentrated so intently on recording the proceedings that she consigned her brief conversation with the woman from the realty company to the back of her mind.

It was thrust to the forefront when Willow went home later for lunch. She sometimes spent a portion of her lunch hour doing the various household chores she hadn't had time to do in the morning. She had mopped the kitchen floor and had just finished waxing it when the telephone shrilled. Willow hovered in the kitchen doorway, reluctant to ruin the floor, but recalling that her mother had promised to let her know the results of tests her father had recently undergone for dizzy spells he'd been having, Willow decided that she had better answer it.

"If it turns out to be a salesman, boy, am I going to be ticked," she muttered as she tiptoed gingerly to the wall phone, her shoes sticking to the wet wax. She lifted the receiver with a rueful glance at the tracks she'd made on the linoleum.

"The receptionist said a woman called for me while I was out. And since you're the only female I know in town, I figured it was probably you," Steven said without preamble.

Willow was glad he couldn't see the guilty color that warmed her cheeks at the sound of his resonant voice. She hadn't reckoned on his powers of deduction and was so disconcerted that she didn't know what to say. She had no intention of admitting that she'd contacted the realty company to verify his employment there and tried to think of a legitimate reason for having made the call. As she hit on one, she conceded, "It was. I wanted to invite you to lunch."

Although Willow had chosen the most expedient course, she didn't like lying. She felt sure that Steven detected the dissembling note in her tone. But as if he noticed nothing out of the ordinary, he said, "I showed a client a piece of property and grabbed something on my way back to the office. Thanks, anyway. Coincidentally, I was planning on getting hold of you to ask if you'd like to go to a movie with me tonight. There's a science fiction film playing. According to the critics, it's a good picture. The visual effects are supposed to be impressive, too. Are you interested?"

Steven named the film, which Willow had been wanting to see since she'd read the reviews. Then, too, she'd been wondering how Steven would react if she told him about Brad's information. She decided that evening would be an excellent opportunity to find out. "Sounds good to me. When?"

THE SCIENCE FICTION FILM proved to be as entertaining as the critics had proclaimed; the visual effects were indeed impressive. As he headed his Jaguar in the direction of Willow's house, Steven said, "The battle between earthlings and the alien invaders was so realistic, it made you feel as if you were right there. Today's technology in filmmaking is really something. Personally, I'm a sucker for the oldies, though, especially the ones they made during the forties and fifties. How about you?"

"Hmm. I'd rather watch those anytime," Willow replied, aware that their taste in movies, like their taste in music, ran along similar lines. Actually, she'd been listening to Steven with only half an ear while contemplating how best to tell him what she had learned from Brad.

Willow had thought about how to broach the subject ever since speaking to Steven earlier in the day, and realized that in all fairness, she couldn't come out with any bold accusations. Granted, she'd done more than hint about her suitcase being searched and the incidents of the prowler, but then she'd had sufficient reason to think him responsible for both. It seemed to her that the current issue should be approached with more diplomacy, at least until she heard what the man had to say for himself.

She had looked for a natural way to interject Brad's news without making it seem that she was grilling Steven, but not having found one, she decided simply to take the plunge. Striving for a nonchalant tone, she said, as if she'd only just thought of it, "I saw Brad Clayton today." She congratulated herself on how casual she sounded. She might have been commenting on the weather, which she noted for the first time that evening was clear, the moon an alabaster crescent, the stars diamond-bright.

"Oh, what's he up to these days?" Steven kept his eyes on the road as he negotiated a sharp corner.

"Nothing much. He was in town on business and dropped by to see me. We got to talking, and your name came up in the conversation. I guess because Brad was the one who introduced us, I thought you and he were friends. But he said he'd never met you before the day Cassie died."

So much for diplomacy, Willow thought with an impatient sigh. In spite of her efforts, her statement had sounded like an accusation. She slanted a look at Steven to gauge whether or not he had taken it as such, but couldn't see his features in the dark.

"Brad hadn't. Neither had the rest of his family," Steven divulged without any prompting. "Somehow I get the feeling you brought him up for a specific reason. Am I right?" Steven shot Willow a sidelong glance and frowned. She'd acted all evening as though she had something on her mind, and now he knew what it was. He thought he could even hazard a guess about where her seemingly offhand remarks were leading.

Following his instincts, he continued. "I remember your saying Cassie'd never said anything about me. You seemed to find it odd. 'Funny,' I think that's the way you put it. So I assume you asked Brad about it and he told you the same thing. Right again?"

Steven was careful to keep his tone level, wryly amused, so that Willow wouldn't guess his true feelings. In reality he was getting damned tired of her suspicions, of the inquisition she'd subjected him to on more than one occasion. He wondered what she would do if he turned the tables on her for once, asked a question or two of his own. Not that he intended to do anything of the kind. It would be too risky. Extreme subtlety was the line to take. Just the same, he couldn't help but wonder.

Willow inwardly cursed Steven's uncanny accuracy. Throwing subterfuge to the winds, she admitted, "Yes. I did ask him. And I still think it's strange that Cassie never told anybody about you." She didn't try to conceal the challenge in her voice.

Having done some quick mental gymnastics, Steven conceded with forced geniality, "I suppose if I were you, I'd probably think so, too. But you mentioned how Cassie's father tried to run her life, and I remember her telling me once he had a habit of investigating some of the people she knew. Maybe she thought he'd do the same to me, so she kept mum about us. I would imagine she got pretty tired of his poking his nose into her personal affairs."

Willow also recalled Cassie's having complained about Addison's investigating some of her acquaintances. He'd evidently had Willow's own family background scrutinized before setting his stamp of approval on Cassie's friendship with her. She remembered how infuriated Cassie had been about it at the time. How indignant her own parents had been! They hadn't cared much for Addison since.

Willow felt rather stupid for not having thought of this explanation herself. Coupled with the knowledge that Steven had told the truth about his job, it caused her to wonder if she'd been wrong about him all along. Perhaps it had been a newspaper reporter who'd rifled through her luggage after all; perhaps the prowler had indeed been a teenager; perhaps Steven's dark apparel that night had merely been a coincidence, as well.

The possibility filled her with sudden contrition. Feeling that an apology was in order, she murmured, "I'm sorry. You'll probably find it hard to believe, but I'm not normally so suspicious. Just the opposite, in fact," she added, recalling how readily she'd swallowed the line of the attorney with whom she'd fallen so impetuously in love. "It's just that there were so many things that seemed—"

"Odd, I know," Steven supplied. "I'm certainly glad we finally worked our way through that." Although he was mollified by Willow's apology, he couldn't resist remarking, "But I'll tell you one thing: If I ever hear the KGB's looking for an interrogator, I'll be sure to give 'em your name." While Willow knew she deserved the barb, she felt her face flame nonetheless.

Still, she owned judiciously that if someone had treated her with such obvious suspicion, she would have been outraged and would have told that person to get irrevocably lost. Surprisingly, however, Steven not only seemed to have taken things in stride, but accepted her peace offering in the form of the brandy he'd declined the night they had dined together. Then when they reached her house, he even indulged Trixie by playing ball with her in the living room while Willow went into the kitchen to pour the liquor.

"I hope you appreciate the honor she's bestowing on you," Willow said. "She doesn't invite everybody to play her favorite game. She'll have you doing it all night if you let her, though, so maybe you should ignore the next pass."

"What, and insult her?" Steven took the brandy snifter Willow handed him as he spoke. "Besides, I think she's already getting tired of it, anyway." Sure enough, Trixie curled up in front of the fireplace.

Steven had removed his jacket and was lounging on the sofa. As Willow sat down beside him, she noticed that the first few buttons of his blue shirt were unfastened. The soft fabric parted to reveal a triangle of dark hair, and she wondered if his entire chest was covered with it, or if he had just enough hair to accentuate his masculinity. Not that it needed accentuating; Willow was more than mildly conscious of the blatant maleness that radiated from him.

She glanced up to find him watching her. A lopsided grin tilted the corners of his mouth, as if he were reading her thoughts. Disconcerted suddenly, she took a quick drink of her brandy. The liquor lodged in her windpipe and she broke into a fit of coughing.

"You okay?" Steven set his brandy snifter down on the coffee table and thumped her on the back. She coughed so hard that she was incapable of speech for a while. When the violent paroxysm passed, Willow looked at him through streaming eyes and nodded.

"Thanks. I guess I swallowed too fast."

A lock of Willow's hair had tumbled down on her forehead, and Steven reached out to gently push it back into place. The gesture was purely impersonal—at least he had intended it to be. But the gardenialike softness of her creamy skin gave sudden life to his fingers. Of their own volition they rested for a fraction of a second on her smooth brow, swept lightly over her temple, then outlined the curve of her high cheekbone, her pointed chin.

Willow's mascara had become slightly streaked, and as Steven wiped away the faint smudges with his thumb, the touch of her tears on his flesh drove an inexplicable shaft of sensation through him. Instantly he pulled his hand away.

Although it was as soft as the brush of a butterfly wing, Steven's touch left a trail of warmth on Willow's skin. His abrupt withdrawal made her feel cold all at once. He'd acted as though his hand had come into contact with a live wire that he couldn't drop quickly enough. She stared at him, bereft of words, her expression bewildered.

Steven summoned a bland smile. "As I recall, you mentioned something once about liking to dance. I scouted around and found a club with a band that plays everything from rock to the big band sound. Want to go there Saturday night?" he asked, in full control of the situation once more.

Willow was thinking that he was the most baffling man she had ever met. One minute he was stroking her face, the next practically pushing her away, then in the next, he behaved as if nothing unusual had happened. She felt flattered that he remembered she enjoyed dancing, however, and thought the date he was proposing might be fun. She started to say yes, then recalled that when returning the candlesticks, Eileen had invited her to dinner that same evening.

Willow explained this to Steven. Then, on impulse, said, "How about if we go dancing another time and you join us Saturday night instead?"

"I don't know. I wouldn't want to intrude."

Steven looked doubtful. Suddenly liking the idea, Willow said encouragingly, "I'm certain my friends wouldn't mind at all. Why don't I give them a jingle right now and see." She glanced at the clock and saw that it was only a little past nine. Aware that Mike and Eileen stayed up to watch the eleven o'clock news, she went into the kitchen to call them.

When Willow asked if she might bring Steven to dinner Saturday evening, Mike said, "Sure, it's fine by me. I think it'll be fine with Eileen, too. She's in the tub, so sit tight while I talk to her." After a brief pause, he returned. "Yeah. It's okay with her. She said something about it giving her a chance to check this guy out. Wouldn't tell me what she meant, but said you'd know. Does this mean our passionate affair's over? That you're actually dumping me for another man?" Mike queried, his deep baritone tinged with humor and mock regret.

"It was great while it lasted. But yes, it's definitely over." Willow assumed the tones of a ruthless old-time movie vamp, Mike retorted that he was sure he would die of a broken heart. Willow was still smiling at

Mike's good-natured teasing when she went back into the living room.

"It's all set. You'll like Mike and Eileen," she predicted as she sat down on the sofa. "They're great people."

"I'm sure I will. . . ."

Steven's response was distracted, and his expression was brooding. Willow wondered what had caused such an abrupt change in his mood again. Guessing that he was still worried about intruding on Mike and Eileen, she assured him, "It really is all right. We'll have a good time, you'll see."

"Oh, I don't have any problem with that. Actually, I was thinking about something else."

"Well, whatever it was, it made you look as if you'd lost your last friend. Want to talk about it? Or should I mind my own business?" Willow asked, torn between discretion and curiosity.

Steven paused to light a cigarette, then said, "I guess your saying you saw Brad Clayton got me to thinking about Cassie. I just realized how lucky we are to be able to go anywhere we want, anytime we want. I was wondering what it would be like to know you're going to be locked away from the rest of the world for twenty years. How did she handle being in prison? I meant to go see her, but never got around to it. Then it was too late."

Steven's critical attitude toward Cassie the first time he'd come to her house had irritated Willow, but the sensitivity he now displayed warmed her. "She didn't handle it very well. It terrified her, naturally. It would have scared anyone who'd never been exposed to that kind of environment, especially somebody who had

lived in the lap of luxury, like Cassie. She hated it—
who wouldn't? Only for her it was worse, I think. She
had a will-o'-the-wisp spirit that led her everywhere
her whims dictated.'' Trixie wandered over to plop
herself down at Willow's feet, and she stroked the
dog's ears, her thoughts on Cassie.

The mixture of sadness and affection etched in
Willow's features caused that earlier inexplicable sensation to surface in Steven again. The fact that he was
still at a complete loss to put a name to it irritated him
all over again. He leaned forward to crush out his half-
smoked cigarette, glad that Willow's attention was
focused on the dog, because he knew his face was set
in a dark scowl. It took him a full minute to wipe the
expression away, and when he had, he picked up the
thread of the conversation.

''I realize how close you and Cassie were. I imagine
you miss her a lot.''

''Yes, and I'll probably go on missing her for a very
long time,'' Willow agreed. As she noticed that his
brandy snifter was empty, she added, ''How about a
refill?''

''No, thanks. I've got an early appointment in the
morning, so I'd better be going.''

As Willow followed Steven into the entry hall, they
made their plans for Saturday evening. He said good-
night, but rather than moving to open the door, he
stared down at her, his dark eyes searching hers intensely, as if he sought the answer to some unspoken
question there. Failing to find whatever he was looking for, he lowered his gaze to her mouth. He studied
it for a long, tense time; then, as though compelled by
some invisible force, Steven lifted his hand to trace the

contour of her lips with his forefinger. He lowered his head until his face was scant inches from Willow's, and her pulses leaped.

Steven's mouth moved toward Willow's until there was nothing between them but the air they breathed. Then, suddenly, he drew away, muttered another good-night, and strode out.

Willow watched his retreating figure, her expression reflecting the conflicting emotions that warred within her. What was wrong with her? She didn't know whether to be disappointed or glad that he hadn't kissed her!

Chapter Seven

Willow's mother contacted her the following after-noon to say that her father's tests had revealed a mild inner ear infection, for which he was being treated. The news came as a relief, and when Saturday ar-rived, Willow found herself looking forward to the evening. Not only because of her fondness for Mike and Eileen, but also because—now that she'd put her suspicions about him aside—Steven would prove to be a much more enjoyable companion.

He turned out to be a charming guest, as well. He was warm and receptive to those around him. He asked questions to draw them out and expressed in-terest in their replies. Mike seemed to like Steven, and that Eileen considered him an attractive male was ap-parent in the approving glances she cast his way. If Steven was aware of her candid evaluation, however, he was too polite to show it.

Eileen remained the perfect hostess until she had served the hors d'oeuvres that accompanied the ex-cellent bottle of wine Steven had provided for the oc-casion. But once in the kitchen, when she and Willow were arranging the stuffed pork chops on a serving dish, Eileen promptly spoke up.

"Good Lord! You said the guy was good-looking, but you didn't say what a gorgeous hunk he is." She pursed her lips in a low, off-key whistle. "Seriously, though, he seems really nice, and I know what you meant when you said it was more likely that women would be looking through his windows. But do you still think he's the one you caught prowling around your place?"

The soft murmur of voices drifted toward the kitchen from the living room, and Willow paused to listen as Steven laughed at something Mike had said. The full-throated richness of the sound produced a tingly vibration along her spine and brought a responsive smile to her lips. "Not anymore. I think the police were probably right about its being kids."

"Well, I'm glad you changed your mind, because I very much approve of him." Eileen sounded like a mother pronouncing judgment on a prospective son-in-law. "This is one of Mike's favorite dishes. I hope Steven likes it, too."

Steven not only seemed to enjoy the pork chops but was highly complimentary about the rest of the meal. Afterward Mike suggested a game of pool in the family room. The pool table was a recent acquisition since Willow had been there last.

"I just got it a few days ago from a guy I work with who's moving to Washington. How about it, you two?" Mike looked from Willow to Steven. "Want to take Eileen and me on? I think before you say yes, though," he said with a vaunting grin, "I'd better warn you I'm pretty good and I've been practicing a lot lately."

"I'm not too bad at it myself," Steven said, his retort a simple statement rather than a boast. "How about you?" he asked Willow. "Ever played?"

Actually, Cassie had taught Willow to shoot pool in the billiard room of the ranch when they were teenagers. A college billiard champion herself, she had been a splendid teacher, Willow a willing pupil who had become quite proficient at the game. Though she hadn't played in years, Willow felt confident that she could still give a good account of herself. Mike's boastful attitude roused the impish side of her nature, however, and she decided to have some fun with them all.

"Once or twice," she answered diffidently. "Only it's been so long, I've probably forgotten how to hold the club." She was hard-pressed to stifle the bubble of laughter that rose to her throat at the pained grimace Steven tried unsuccessfully to conceal.

The self-assured gleam in Mike's eyes clearly showed that he had dismissed her as a negligible opponent, and Willow aimed a mischievous grin at his back as he led the way into the family room.

"What'll it be, folks? Straight pool or eight ball?"

The former was the unanimous choice, and a toss of a coin determined that Steven and Willow would start the game. Willow had a momentary stab of guilt when Steven patiently delayed the action to illustrate the proper way in which to position the cue stick. The balls were racked. Mike broke them and with a smug smile stepped aside so that Willow could make the initial shot.

First Willow walked around the table to study the clustered balls, as Cassie had taught her to do. Next she took up her stance, positioned her cue stick, and, focusing her concentration on the cue and object balls, gently stroked the cue ball to nudge the three-ball into a corner pocket. Calling her shots before each play, she went on to sink five of the six remaining solid balls, conscious of Mike's deflated expression, Steven's openmouthed astonishment and Eileen's wide-eyed surprise.

"Oh, brother! 'I've probably forgotten how to hold the club,'" Eileen quoted when Willow paused to chalk the end of her cue stick. "I think we've been hoodwinked, guys. Looks to me like we've got a real live Minnesota Fats on our hands. You little stinker," she chided Willow good-naturedly.

"Nevada Slim," Steven corrected her, his pointed gaze sliding with slow deliberation over Willow's figure. Her red jumpsuit hugged her slender body in all the right places, he noticed, and her gamine grin did odd things to his senses. "But you're right, Eileen. We've definitely been hoodwinked. You're doing great," he encouraged Willow. "Now sink the other two and run the table."

Whether because of Steven's provocative look or because of overconfidence, Willow failed to make the next shot, and Steven pocketed the final balls to win the game.

Willow soon discovered that Steven's belief that he could hold his own was no idle boast. The skill he demonstrated pleased and impressed her. Mike played relatively well himself but had a tendency to blast into the balls, imparting too much spin, while Eileen was given to sinking the white cue ball, which caused her and Mike to lose points. Steven and Willow won six games out of six, all of which elicited good-humored grumbling from Mike and Eileen.

When they had completed the last game, Mike turned to Willow with a sheepish look, rubbing his chin. "See anything yellow?" he asked. "That's funny. I could've sworn I had egg all over my face. But if we ever play again, it'll either be Steve and me against you gals, or I'll have you on my side."

"Why, you dirty devil!" Eileen punched him playfully on the arm. Mike let it hang limply, pretending she had broken it.

Since the distance between the two houses was a short one, Willow hadn't bothered to wear a coat, and when she and Steven said their goodbyes and stepped outside, the frigid air went through her gabardine jumpsuit. She wasn't aware until they reached her house that her nipples had tautened and were pushing against the fabric. Steven's gaze clung with undisguised male interest to the stiff peaks. Suddenly arrested by his concentrated study, she stood in the center of the living room and stared at him. When he realized that she was staring back at him, he wrested his glance away. "You're cold. I'll build a fire."

Willow felt quite warm all at once, as if her entire body were flushed. But rather than argue the point, she sank down on the sofa while Steven assembled the ingredients for a fire. When he had a cheerful blaze going, he joined her there.

"I told you Eileen and Mike were fun people, didn't I?" Willow smiled at him, noting how the firelight lent an amber glow to his bronzed skin.

"Yes, and you were right. They're good sports, too. But tell me, does your being so good at pool have anything to do with Cassie's having been the college billiard champ two years in a row?" Steven gave her a knowing grin as he crossed one long leg over the other. He brushed his muscular thigh against hers as he did so, and the contact flooded her with warmth once more.

"Uh-huh. She taught me, and we played every chance we got whenever I was at the ranch. Cassie was proud of her skill, even if her father had visions of her disgracing the family by becoming a pool hustler. I wish you could've seen your face when I called the cue stick a club, though." Willow chuckled reminiscently. "I really had you worried there for a while, didn't I?"

"You sure did. Only now you've got me wondering if there's anything else you've neglected to tell me about yourself." Despite his light tone, Steven's eyes probed Willow's as deeply as they had on the night they'd gone to the movies, again seeking the reply to some unspoken question.

Suddenly curious, she frowned and said, "You know, you've looked at me that same way before. In fact..."

"What way?" Steven countered, having changed his expression to one of mild inquiry.

"I'm not exactly sure. But it's like there's some-thing about me you can't figure out. Is there?" Wil-low leaned away slightly so that she could scan his face.

Her observation was more astute than she realized. But Steven knew that to admit she was right would be sheer stupidity. Because not only would he tip his

hand, he would blow the lid off the whole thing before he was ready. He'd always prided himself on
having a poker face, but now he had to glance aside,
chiding himself for having given his thoughts away, to
frame a suitable reply.

"Not really. It's just that you seem to be a lady of
surprises. Tonight, for instance, I fully expected us to
get trounced, and we ended up beating the pants off
Mike and Eileen. I just thought you might have some
other tricks up your sleeve. How are you at skeet
shooting, archery, tennis, for example?"

"I've never tried the first two, and my tennis game
is only average. Why? Are you one of those chauvin-
istic men who can't stand to be beaten by a woman?"
Willow teased.

"Not at all. I only thought if you were good at any
of those, I'd get in some practice before I went up
against you." A crooked smile played across his features as he went on to say something else. But rather
than listening, Willow found herself watching his
mouth. It was firm, well defined, the lower lip full,
sensual. She wondered what it would feel like on her
own.

She went on gazing at it with hypnotized fascination, her concentration so keen that she wasn't aware
at which precise point Steven had stopped speaking.
She was conscious only of the sudden pulsating silence that beat between them, of Steven's glance
trained on her own lips. Willow guessed by his com-
prehending look that he had read her thoughts again.
Disconcerted all at once, she started to shift position
but grew still when something flickered in his eyes.

Whatever it was, it fled in the next instant, replaced by indecision. Then this vanished as well, and Steven reached out to cup Willow's chin in his hand. Slowly yet inexorably he drew nearer, so near that Willow glimpsed the pulse that throbbed in his temple before his mouth claimed hers in a kiss that was tentative at first. Then, as he explored the unknown territory of her lips, the pressure of his mouth deepened, and his hand left her face to gather her into his arms.

Steven's kiss was more arousing than anything Willow could have imagined. A surge of pure pleasure spread over her when he created an entry with his tongue to chart a titillating course through the moistened interior of her mouth. Without volition, Willow's fingers glided up over the nape of his neck to entangle themselves in the soft strands of his hair.

She returned his kiss and gasped in mingled surprise and delight as his mouth left hers to move leisurely down the velvety column of her throat. His tongue darted out to taste the perfumed hollow for a delectable moment before his lips fastened on hers once more with a kiss of such shattering intensity that it sent the blood rushing to her head.

Willow felt immersed in a pool of delightful sensation from which she found herself reluctant to surface. She gave a protesting moan when he unfastened his mouth from hers once more to raise his head fractionally. He peered into her languorous eyes for another long moment. Then, with a ragged sigh, he pulled her across him until she was half lying, her body supported by his arm.

Willow's hands explored the rippling muscles of Steven's back, the heat from him sending shock waves through her questing fingertips. Unconcealed desire transformed his eyes to burning ebony, and she pressed closer when his hand wandered downward to cup her breast. It was only as he slid down the zipper of her jumpsuit, unhooked her lacy bra and began to stroke her bare flesh that sanity suddenly returned.

Willow recalled with sickening clarity that her relationship with the attorney with whom she'd fallen in love so quickly had begun in just the same way. Within a week of their first meeting they had begun sleeping together on a regular basis. Her firm determination to take future romantic involvements slowly caused her to utter another moan of protest as Steven's mouth whispered down to follow the path of his hand. The knowledge that she herself had initiated the intimate scene flooded her face with color. Abruptly she released herself, aware of Steven's confused expression before she turned away.

"It's still cold in here. The fire must be going out." In reality the crackling blaze made the room excessively hot, almost stuffy, but Willow needed some excuse to allow herself time to adjust her clothing and regain her composure. Adding another log, she wondered what Steven thought about her having acted like a love-starved maniac one minute and a nervous virgin the next. She slid a sidelong glance at him through veiled lashes as she closed the meshed fireplace screen, but saw nothing to indicate his reaction.

Steven caught Willow's covert look and strove to keep his features blank. He hadn't intended to kiss her; he'd done so only because she'd so obviously wanted him to. Not that he hadn't been tempted, and he knew he'd be a damned liar to deny he'd enjoyed holding her in his arms and feeling her moist mouth beneath his. Still, kissing was part of the dating ritual and to all intents and purposes that was why he was there. He had no idea why Willow had broken away from him so suddenly, but he was glad just the same. She had a way of making mincemeat out of the discipline he'd learned over the years, and he had a feeling he was going to have his work cut out for him to be sure he didn't fall into a trap of his own making.

Willow decided she would only become more embarrassed if she tried to explain her ambivalent behavior. As she sat down again on the other end of the sofa, she struggled for a way to breach the uncomfortable silence that had followed her abrupt retreat. Belatedly remembering her manners, she offered Steven some refreshment.

"I'm still stuffed from dinner." He patted his flat belly. His hair was ruffled from the gentle torment of Willow's fingers, and as if in realization, he smoothed his palm over the thick dark mane. Another lengthy pause fell between them, during which time he appeared to be contemplating something. Then he said, "I heard on the car radio on my way here that it's supposed to be nice tomorrow. I've got a Piper Cherokee 180 I use for long trips. I'm planning on flying it to San Francisco in the morning. Would you like to go, too?"

Although Willow hadn't been there for several years, she loved the fascinating places to visit and the melting pot of cultures San Francisco provided. She accepted eagerly, and before he left, Steven advised her

to wear comfortable shoes, as they would undoubtedly do a good deal of walking.

They took off bright and early from the Carson City
airport for the two-hour flight. Willow had flown only
on larger commercial aircraft, and she had a slight
sensation of claustrophobia from the small airplane,
but once they were soaring high above the snow-
capped Sierras, she forgot about it and settled back to
enjoy the trip. The skill with which Steven handled the
controls assured her that he was an expert pilot.

Once in San Francisco, he proved to be an engag-
ing escort, leading Willow on pleasurable excursions
to art galleries, museums, and the Japanese Tea Gar-
dens near Golden Gate Park. In Chinatown, from
where they rode one of the charming old-world cable
cars to Fishermen's Wharf, he bought her a lovely
ivory fan on which she had cast admiring eyes. Together they absorbed the intriguing sights and sounds
unique to San Francisco. Then later, when he returned her home, Steven left her with the promise of
"Be seeing you."

AND SEE HER HE DID. During the next two weeks Steven took Willow bowling, to another play and to a
figure-skating exhibition in Reno. Sometimes when on
chilly evenings they decided to stay in, he brought
classic movies from his extensive library to watch on
her VCR. As Willow got to know him better, she discovered that they shared a mutual passion for Italian
food and a decided preference for the work of the Renaissance artists and the haunting poetry of Yeats.

Steven kissed her often, and though his touch filled
her with increasing pleasure, Willow's resolution to

allow their budding relationship to develop at a grad-
ual pace kept her from letting the situation get out of
hand. Then, too, while she sensed that Steven was
strongly attracted to her, he seemed reluctant to let
their association progress to a more intimate level.
Although Willow wasn't quite certain about his reasons, she was content to take things one step at a time.

All in all, those two weeks were the most pleasant
she could remember having spent in a very long time,
so much so that she experienced a sharp pang of disappointment when he announced he was going to
Utah for a few days. He made the announcement on
a Saturday night when he took her dancing at the club
he had told her about earlier. Coincidentally, the ten-
piece band was playing "Sentimental Journey." As
they glided together across the dance floor, Steven
said, "They must've had me in mind when they chose
that. I'll leave tomorrow and probably be back Tuesday or Wednesday sometime."

He didn't say if his trip was for business or personal reasons, and despite her curiosity, Willow re-
frained from asking. Steven had spoken freely about
himself, so she knew he wouldn't have minded her
asking. She simply didn't want him to think her a
possessive female who insisted on knowing the every
move of the man she was dating.

To hide her disappointment, Willow gave him a
bright smile. "Are you planning on flying your plane
to Utah?"

She tilted her head back so that she could look up
at him, and his warm breath fanned her hair as he replied, "You bet. It beats driving, even if the sky's so
crowded they're going to have to put in stop signs at

all the major intersections. Umm, listen, one of my favorites,'' Steven murmured when the nostalgic strains of another popular old tune reached them from the bandstand.

He drew Willow closer. Nestling her cheek against his shoulder, she noted how fragile her small hand curled in his large palm appeared. The mingled scents of soap and after-shave teased her nostrils, and the arm that encircled her slender waist suggested a sinewy strength yet was gentle. As Steven propelled her to a less populated section of the floor, their perfectly matched steps belied the fact that this was the first time they had danced together. Willow liked the sinuous grace with which he moved to the standard songs, the uninhibited way he gyrated to the soul-shaking beat of the current rock hits.

They danced to every tune and remained until the place closed.

Afterward, heading toward her house in the Jaguar, and discussing the versatility of the musicians, Willow noticed that Steven was giving occasional glances at the rearview mirror. At first she set these intermittent looks down to nothing more than alert driving, but when they became an almost constant stare, she grew so inquisitive that she twisted around to look behind them. When she saw nothing but the mild stream of late-night traffic, she turned back to Steven.

''Is something wrong?''

Steven drew the car to a halt at a red light, and through the diffused glow of a streetlamp, Willow saw the heavy frown that scored the area between his eyebrows. ''I'm not sure. But unless I'm mistaken, we're being followed and have been since shortly after we left the club.''

"Really?" As Willow craned her head around to look behind them again, she spied a gray sedan with a man at the wheel. Instead of closing the distance between the two automobiles, he persistently left a wide gap, making it impossible for her to make out his features. His apparent desire to remain unidentified struck Willow as remarkably suspicious. She asked with a sudden sense of uneasiness, "Why would he be following *us*?" She kept her eyes trained on the other car, the harsh glare of its headlights in the back window causing her to squint.

"I have no idea. Unless it's a jealous boyfriend of yours wanting to know who you've been keeping company with lately," Steven said in a half-teasing, half-serious tone.

Willow's feminine pride precluded her from admitting that other than Steven, she had no boyfriends at the moment, jealous or otherwise, so she said simply, "None of the men I date would act so immaturely. Besides, nobody I know drives a gray sedan."

Steven's assumption that Willow could make men jealous made her forget her uneasiness for an instant. It came flooding back in the next when he speculated, "The only other thing I can think of is, maybe he spotted this car and decided we'd be an easy mark for robbery." The light turned green, and he eased the Jaguar forward. "If that's what he's planning, he picked the wrong guy to try it on. Hold on. I'm going to see if he really is tailing us, then if he is, give him the slip."

They were approaching the avenue on which Willow lived. But rather than turning there, Steven continued along North Carson Street. Several blocks farther on, he made an abrupt U-turn at an intersection. Her attention still fixed on the rear window, Willow watched as the driver of the gray sedan repeated the maneuver and heard an angry blast on the horn from the truck he cut in front of before he trailed after the Jaguar.

The knowledge that he was indeed following them heightened her apprehension, and she gasped when Steven executed a sudden right turn and almost sideswiped a van parked along the curb. The other car swung down the same street, and Steven downshifted to gain speed as he negotiated a left turn with such sharpness that the tires squealed in protest. Willow clutched the edge of the dashboard so tightly that her knuckles began to hurt. Her jawbone ached from clenching her teeth to prevent herself from crying out when a black cat suddenly streaked across their path.

Tension-charged silence prevailed as Steven made a series of right and left turns into narrow streets designed for sedate driving instead of the Indianapolis 500 speedway tactics he was using. As Willow flicked a look at him, she glimpsed the rigid set of his jaw, the fierce concentration on his face. He darted a glance into the rearview mirror again, and his features relaxed, triumph chasing away his heavy frown.

Willow peered over her shoulder through the rear window once more. No headlights penetrated the blackness behind them, proof Steven had indeed eluded their pursuer. Either that, Willow reasoned, or the driver of the gray sedan, realizing Steven knew he was being followed, had decided not to try anything after all. To make certain the other driver had given up the pursuit, Steven pulled the Jaguar to a stop in front of a darkened house, cut the engine and lights, then waited. When several minutes passed without any sign of another vehicle, Willow gave a sigh of relief. She hadn't realized until then that she had maintained her viselike grip on the rim of the dashboard. She pried her fingers away and rubbed them vigorously to restore the circulation.

"Wow! You came so close to hitting that cat, I could have sworn I saw its fur fly! Do you really think that guy would've robbed us if he'd gotten the chance?"

"That's something we'll probably never know. But we'll keep a sharp eye peeled for him, just in case he's still hanging around somewhere."

"And if he is?" Willow asked as Steven started the car again.

"I'll pull him over and confront him this time," Steven retorted, his tone fraught with steely determination.

"But that could be dangerous. What if he's got a knife or a gun? He could shoot you before you even got out of the car," Willow objected, her former nervousness returning twofold.

"I've never had any trouble defending myself when the need arises. So I'll worry about that if and when it happens." Steven delivered both statements with such male complacence that at any other time Willow would have accused him of boasting. As it was, his bold assurance failed to banish the mixture of trepidation and dread that assailed her at the possibility of a confrontation between him and the driver of the gray sedan.

Fortunately, Willow's fears went unrealized. Neither the quiet residential neighborhoods, nor the noisier casino-strewn downtown district harbored the other car, and they reached Willow's house some minutes later without having seen it again. Relief washed over her once more, and she decided to put the occurrence out of her mind.

Steven wouldn't come into the house. "Not tonight, thanks. I want to get an early start in the morning and I've still got to pack," he said, unlocking the front door. He put the key ring into Willow's hand, then took her into his arms for a long, lingering kiss, which immediately sent her blood singing through her veins. Willow laced her fingers around his neck, her body unconsciously melting into Steven's as his mouth left hers to rove slowly over her hair, eyes, cheeks, throat, as if he wanted to carry the taste of her with him while he was away. He kissed her again. Willow suddenly experienced the same desire, and her lips became the parted petals of a flower that open wide to drink in delicious drops of morning dew. She savored him as he savored her, and when at last he released her, she emerged from the final kiss limp and shaken.

Willow whispered a breathy, "Good night. Have a safe trip," and on legs that quivered slightly, slipped inside. Her lips still tingling from the exciting plunder of Steven's mouth, she padded toward the bedroom, a sleepy-eyed Trixie trailing along behind.

Steven paused on the porch to light a cigarette, his mind on Willow's obvious disappointment at the news of his trip. Actually he wasn't planning on going to

Utah or anywhere else. He had invented a trip because he'd felt an urgent need to be alone in order to put things into proper perspective and focus his energies on his main objective, both of which were becoming increasingly difficult when Willow was near. She acted on him like an insidious drug, seduced his senses and could be detrimental to reaching his goal. He had known getting romantically involved with her would be a calculated risk, but under the circumstances, he hadn't seen any other way to proceed without arousing her suspicions again. Putting some distance between him and Willow, he hoped, would get him back on the right track. If it didn't . . .

But Steven refused to dwell on negatives. With a sudden flick of his wrist, he tossed away his half-smoked cigarette, which was ground under his heel as he strode to his car. Once behind the wheel, he forcibly transferred his thoughts from Willow to the gray sedan. Despite his having theorized that the other driver had planned a roadside robbery, he wondered now if he and Willow had been followed for an entirely different reason.

Though Steven hadn't the slightest idea what that reason might be, the incident had caused his intuition to stir. It was still deeply uneasy long after he had driven away.

Chapter Eight

Although Willow had known she enjoyed Steven's company, she hadn't realized how accustomed she'd become in the past couple of weeks to having him around. Nor had she anticipated the void the absence of his vital presence created, the creeping boredom that settled over her without him there to share her leisure time. To relieve the monotony, she caught up on her reading, worked on crossword puzzles and scrubbed every inch of her house until it gleamed like a newly minted coin. And still she was unspeakably bored.

On the third day after Steven's departure two things happened that temporarily broke the tedium of Willow's solitary evenings.

Generally she paid her monthly household bills as soon as she received them, but they had slipped her mind, and it wasn't until Tuesday evening that she remembered them. After dinner she went to get the bills down from a drawer in the maple hutch where she kept them. As soon as she entered the dining room, she noticed that the dollhouse, which normally faced directly outward, was turned sideways, and the twin doors at the rear stood wide open, as well. A bewildered frown knitting her brow, Willow wondered how it had gotten into that peculiar position. She recalled having dusted everything in the dining room, including the dollhouse, during her recent housecleaning spree. Perhaps she had unconsciously left it that way. She could have sworn she hadn't, but since she'd been the only person in the house for the past few days, she must have done.

With a shrug, Willow closed the doors and turned the dollhouse back to its rightful position, collected the bills and carried them to the kitchen table, where she spent the next half hour filling out checks.

While Willow grudgingly conceded that bill paying was a necessary part of life, she found it irritating and was always glad when it was finished, so the shrill of the telephone that came as she put her signature to the last check was uncommonly welcome.

"Hello," she said with a smile that matched her cheerful tone, then said it again when she was met by silence. If someone had dialed the wrong number and was too disconcerted to say so, the other party would have hung up. But the line stayed open, and as Willow listened more closely, she heard the distinct sound of heavy breathing. Whoever it was had a cold, or else...

The one and only obscene call Willow had ever received had begun in just such a way. Still, to give the person the benefit of the doubt, she said, "Hello" again. Once more she heard only heavy breathing and decided to scare the hell out of her caller.

"Look," she said sternly, "I don't know if you got this number by mistake, but this is the sheriff's house, and we record all incoming calls. You're being taped right now.''

Willow inwardly congratulated herself on the speed of her invention. She felt certain the unknown person would sever the connection and waited for the sharp click that would signal he had done so. Strangely, he responded with a muffled chuckle of such sinister content that a tinge of apprehension crept over her. The motion purely spontaneous, she slammed down the phone.

Her fingers hovered over the receiver as she analyzed that muted mirth. It seemed to suggest that the caller not only knew exactly whom he had reached, but also was amused by her lie. She decided not to answer the telephone if it rang again. But it was silent.

THE NEXT CALL she received at home was from Steven, the following afternoon during her lunch hour. Willow's pulse set up an instant hammering when she recognized his rumbling baritone. He invited her to a casino in Reno that evening to see a popular female rock star perform. Willow had mentioned once that the star was her favorite singer, and she thought it was sweet of him to have remembered.

"I know it's short notice," Steven said, "but I just got the tickets. This is her last night, and the later performances are sold out. The only ones I could get are for the dinner show. It starts at seven, so I'll pick you up at your place around six. How's that for you?"

"Not good. A lawyer I know asked me to come by his office after work to take a deposition for a client. I said I'd be there a little after five."

"Any chance of getting out of it?"

"Afraid not. He needs the deposition for a trial tomorrow morning. I won't have much time to go home and dress." Willow pursed her lips thoughtfully as she did some fast mental calculations. After a moment she suggested, "How about instead of you picking me up here, we meet somewhere? I'll bring my clothes with me to work and change there. That'll save time."

"Good idea." Steven mentioned a bar on the north end of town, and since Willow wasn't sure precisely when she would get there, they arranged to meet inside.

She wanted to look especially beautiful for him that evening, so she decided to take a black satin-and-lace dress and the proper accessories with her to work.

It was six o'clock by the time she left the lawyer's office. Instead of feeling beautiful, she felt more like a hastily made bed. She suppressed a rueful sigh as she backed the Camaro out of her parking space. The bar where she was to meet Steven was ten minutes away, and she swept along the icy streets faster than she normally drove.

Though she had never been there, she had heard the place was popular with the singles crowd. From all appearances, that was no idle rumor. Despite the fact that it was a week night, the parking lot was jammed to overflowing. Consequently, Willow had to park across the street. She had seen Steven's Jaguar near the entrance and knew that he was waiting inside. Aware of the half-hour drive still ahead of them, she stepped out quickly and locked the doors. Another vehicle pulled up behind hers, but she hardly noticed. Anxious to let Steven know she had arrived, she turned

away from her car, the throbbing engine of the other
vehicle a low hum in her ears.

Willow didn't know if the strange feeling that suddenly enveloped her was a premonition. But as she
started across the street, something compelled her to
pause and look behind her. What she saw caused incredulous shock to widen her eyes, and her heart to
give a sudden lurch.

Someone wearing a yellow ski mask, which covered face and hair, was bearing down on her with a
swift, purposeful stride. Willow assumed the person
was a man, from the stocky build and khaki pants, but
her attention was riveted on the object he carried in his
hand. It gleamed menacingly in a vagrant shaft of
moonlight.

Invisible tentacles of fear wrapped around Willow
as she realized she was looking at a knife. She stiff-
ened, her body transformed to marble, incapable of
movement. She tried to scream, but her mouth merely
formed a silent O and no sound came out. Then the
same fear that had immobilized her only a second before abruptly galvanized her into action.

She whirled and fled across the street toward the
side entrance of the bar. The tight skirt of her dress
hampered her progress, and she used both hands to
hike it up over her knees, dropping her black sequined evening bag in the process. She heard the
sound of running feet and knew that the masked man
was rapidly closing in on her. The bone-chilling
knowledge increased her speed, while panic caused her
breath nearly to burst from her laboring lungs. The
bar loomed before her; the tubular neon lights

HARLEQUIN GIVES YOU SIX REASONS TO CELEBRATE!

INCLUDING

**1.
4 FREE
BOOKS**

**2.
AN ELEGANT
MANICURE SET**

**3.
A SURPRISE
BONUS**

AND MORE!

TAKE A LOOK . . .

Yes, become a Harlequin home subscriber and the celebration goes on forever.

To begin with we'll send you:

- **4 new Harlequin Intrigue novels** – Free
- **an elegant, purse-size manicure set** – Free
- **and an exciting mystery bonus** – Free

And that's not all! Special extras – Three more reasons to celebrate

4. Money-Saving Home Delivery That's right! When you become a Harlequin home subscriber the excitement, romance and far-away adventures of Harlequin Intrigue novels can be yours for previewing in the convenience of your own home **at less than retail prices.** Here's how it works. Every other month we'll deliver four new books right to your door. If you decide to keep them, they'll be yours for only $1.99! That's 26¢ less per book than what you pay in stores. And there is **no charge for shipping and handling.**

5. Free Newsletter - It's "Heart to Heart" – **the** indispensable insider's look at our most popular writers and their up-coming novels. Now you can have a behind-the-scenes look at the fascinating world of Harlequin! It's an added bonus you'll look forward to every other month!

6. More Surprise Gifts – Because our home subscribers are our most valued readers, we'll be sending you additional free gifts from time to time – as a token of our appreciation.

This beautiful manicure set will be a useful and elegant item to carry in your handbag. Its rich burgundy case is a perfect expression of your style and good taste. And it's yours free in this amazing Harlequin celebration!

HARLEQUIN READER SERVICE
FREE OFFER CARD

4 FREE BOOKS

ELEGANT MANICURE SET – FREE

FREE MYSTERY BONUS

PLACE YOUR BALLOON STICKER HERE!

MONEY SAVING HOME DELIVERY

FREE FACT-FILLED NEWSLETTER

MORE SURPRISE GIFTS THROUGHOUT THE YEAR – FREE

☐ **YES!** Please send me my four Harlequin Intrigue novels **Free**, along with my manicure set and my **free mystery gift**. Then send me four new Harlequin Intrigue novels every other month and bill me just $1.99 per book (26¢ less than retail), with no extra charges for shipping and handling. If I am not completely satisfied, I may return a shipment and cancel at any time. **The free books, manicure set and mystery gift remain mine to keep.**   180 CII RDAF

FIRST NAME _____ LAST NAME _____
(PLEASE PRINT)

ADDRESS _____ APT. _____

CITY _____ STATE _____

ZIP _____

Prices subject to change. Offer limited to one per household and not valid to present subscribers.

HARLEQUIN "NO RISK GUARANTEE"
- There is no obligation to buy – the free books and gifts remain yours to keep.
- You pay the lowest price possible – and receive books before they're available in stores.
- You may end your subscription anytime-just let us know.

PRINTED IN U.S.A.

Remember! To receive your four free books,
manicure set and surprise mystery bonus return the
postpaid card below. But don't delay!

DETACH & MAIL CARD TODAY

If card has been removed, write to: Harlequin Reader Service,
901 Fuhrmann Blvd., P.O. Box 1394, Buffalo, NY 14240-1394

mounted on its roof were fingers beckoning her to safety. Safety that Willow never attained.

The instant her flying feet struck the sidewalk, her long hair was snatched from behind and her pursuer hauled her roughly back against him. Needles of fire shot through her scalp, and her pain-filled shriek was abruptly cut off by a hand that clamped over her mouth. The force was so brutal that her teeth ground into the inside of her lip. A salty ribbon of blood trickled over Willow's tongue as he pinioned her left arm to her side and thrust the sharp knife point into the flesh beneath her jawbone.

"Just do what you're told and nothing will happen to you," he ordered, his gravelly voice a harsh rasp. Her arm still imprisoned at her side, he propelled her back across the street. Another scream welled up inside her, but his bruising grip on her mouth kept it trapped in her throat. Willow prayed that someone would come along and intervene, but the street and sidewalks were deserted, as though she and her captor were the only two people left alive in the world. She had no choice but to comply when he forced her between the two cars and made her open the passenger door of his vehicle.

"We're going for a ride and you're going to drive," he said over the humming engine.

For the first time Willow noticed the color of his car. She instantly recognized it as the gray sedan that had followed her and Steven the night he'd taken her dancing. Contrary to Steven's speculation about robbery, she alone had been the man's intended victim. But why? What did he want with her?

Rape. Murder. The frightening possibilities sent the blood rushing to her head to beat a wild tattoo against her skull. Willow was conscious only that once she got into the sedan she would be completely at his mercy. She must do everything in her power to stay out of the car.

With a swiftness born of pure terror, she shoved her right elbow into his ribs and simultaneously ground her stiletto heel into his instep with all the strength she could muster. His enraged curse mingled with Willow's cry of pain as he hurled her into the car with such force that she hit her forehead on the door-frame. She sprawled momentarily across the front seat, her senses swimming from the impact. Then she heaved her body against the other door, her fingers grappling frantically with the handle in a desperate bid for freedom. The scream that had been denied her tore from her throat. But the street remained deserted, her attempt to escape doomed to failure. Her assailant lunged at her, the knife point biting into her jugular vein.

"Turn the car around and head for Reno."

Once more Willow had to obey. As she left the safety of the bar behind, her legs trembled so violently that she had difficulty keeping her foot from slipping off the gas pedal. She swallowed convulsively to rid her mouth of the acrid taste of terror, but it only grew stronger when the lights of town faded into the darkness. Her voice was thin, reedy as she asked the questions that tormented her fear-ridden brain.

"Wh-where are you taking me? What d-do you want?"

"Just shut up and drive. You'll find out when we get there." The last remark contained the hint of a threat, and in spite of the warmth her rabbit coat provided, Willow shook even more violently. This time when the man spoke, though, she realized she had heard that gruff voice before. It seemed vaguely familiar, but when she tried to put a face to it, she drew a blank. She filed it away in the back of her mind, and her heart plunged to the floorboards as they reached the highway.

Willow had hoped to find it busy, so that she could honk the horn to alert someone to her danger, but the traffic was thin. The only vehicles she saw were shooting by on the opposite side of the highway. Farther on she spotted a deep trench to her right and toyed with the idea of running the sedan into it. But she was afraid that her abductor might anticipate her intention and stab her before she could carry it out.

Although he retained his grasp on the knife, he had laid it against his knee rather than holding it at Willow's throat. That failed to diminish her terror, which reached monumental proportions when, about fifteen minutes later, he ordered her to turn off the highway. At his command, she drove down a winding dirt road in a westerly direction, the distant snow-covered hills milky mounds that stood out in bold relief against the inky sky. The surrounding terrain was stark, desolate. The few misshapen manzanita bushes, scrub oaks and pines that sprouted up out of the flat landscape reminded Willow of unsightly growths. She pried her gaze away and looked straight ahead.

They continued down the unpaved road for several miles until she was instructed to turn onto another dirt

track, which branched to the left. The area was remote, devoid of any sign of civilization. Willow wondered what lay at the end of the track. Then the
headlights struck a dimly lit shack, which jutted up
from out of nowhere. As they drew near she could see
that it was small and badly run down. The sight of it
frightened her almost as much as her knife-wielding
abductor, because she knew that whatever he planned
to do to her, he would do it there.

The horrific knowledge caused icy rivulets of perspiration to stream down her face. Until then her mind
had been too mired in fear to allow for clear thinking.
As he instructed her to stop the sedan on the other side
of the shack, however, she decided to try to reason
with him.

Willing her voice not to quaver, she said, "I don't
know if you're aware of it, but kidnapping carries a
pretty stiff penalty. You could get years, even life, if
you're caught."

"I don't plan on that happening. So cut the crap
and get out of the car!" he snapped, plainly not in the
least intimidated. Willow considered making a break
for it, but he was on her in a flash, the knife pressed
into her back. He marched her into the cabin. It contained only a narrow cot, a rickety chair and an up-
ended orange crate in a corner. A kerosene lamp on
the crate cast a harsh glow on the Spartan furnishings. "Now, Miss Laughlin, you and I are gonna have
a talk. Sit down!" He pushed her toward the chair,
which stood in the center of the crude wooden floor.
The use of Willow's surname confirmed the fact that
he knew her, even if she still couldn't recall where she
had heard his voice before.

It grew even more raspy when he added, "I need some information. So you can tell me what I want to know voluntarily or I can force it out of you. Doesn't matter to me either way." His indifferent shrug emphasized the breadth of his shoulders beneath the plaid wool jacket.

The unveiled threat conjured an image of torture so vivid that Willow shuddered. With the last remark, he moved to the cot, laid down his knife and picked up a short length of rope. Realizing that he was going to tie her to the chair and she would be totally at his mercy unless she did something to prevent it, Willow determined to resist him with every ounce of strength she possessed.

He looked as strong as a bull, and Willow was aware that he could easily overpower her. She decided to use surprise. A thread of a thought unraveled in her mind and she swiftly wove it into a plan. Striving for a defeated tone, she said, "Since you're calling the shots, there's nothing I can do but cooperate." While she was faintly curious about the information he desired, she didn't comment on it. She wanted her mind free of distraction in order to implement her scheme.

"Right. I'm glad you finally realized that. Save us both a lot of hassle." He came toward her as he spoke, the rope stretched between his hands. Willow watched him, her senses honed to a sharp pitch, her body as taut as a tightly coiled spring. When he got within a couple of feet of her, she suddenly catapulted from the chair and rushed at him, using her lowered head to butt him in the stomach.

The unexpected maneuver knocked the wind out of him and sent the rope snaking to the floor. His explosive breath sounded like an erupting volcano in the silent shack. Willow caught a glimpse of the angry glitter in his eyes through the slits of his mask a second before he seized her to hurl her back into the chair.

His fingers bit cruelly into her shoulders, but she ignored the pain. She struggled with all her might, jackknifed her leg to knee him in the groin, pummeled his masked face with her fists. His enraged "Bitch!" reverberated like a pistol shot, but he did not slacken his hold on her shoulders. Willow thought he would grind her bones into dust. Still she fought him, yet for all the fear-induced fury with which she did so, she might as well have been a flea battling an elephant.

Though her strength was dwindling fast, Willow refused to give in. She reached up to claw his eyes and kicked his shin at the same time. He anticipated her intentions and twisted his head back. His ski mask came away in Willow's hand and tumbled from her nerveless fingers, unnoticed.

Her shocked gasp hissed in her throat as she stared at the exposed face of her kidnapper. She realized then why his voice had sounded familiar. She had indeed heard it before, and had seen his meaty features several times when she'd visited Cassie in prison. He was Frank Fielding, the guard who had sent her the dollhouse.

He had always behaved sympathetically toward the inmates in his charge. Even as he stared back at Willow, she imagined she saw an underlining hint of regret beneath the rage that contorted his face. "I went to a helluva lot of trouble so you wouldn't identify me.

Too bad you didn't leave it that way. I only brought you here to scare you. But now..."

The words hung suspended in the air, ominous, frightening, foreboding. Menace filled his face, and fresh terror sluiced over Willow. She knew that the moment she had torn off his mask she had inadvertently signed her own death warrant.

Chapter Nine

Willow swallowed a strangled sob that spiraled up from the wellspring of her being. It occurred to her with panic-stricken irony that Fielding was going to kill her and she didn't even know why he had abducted her. Perhaps she could delay the inevitable until she could think of something to save herself.

Unable to control her trembling voice, she asked, "Why did you kidnap me?"

"Because you were the last one Cassandra Clayton talked to before she died. I figured she told you where the money from the robbery was. It's no good to you now, so you might as well tell—"

"But I don't know where it is. Cassie never said anything about it," Willow cut in without thinking. Too late she realized her mistake. Instead of blurting out the truth, she should have strung him along, invented some mythical place where the money was hidden, forced him to take her there. That would have bought her some time, perhaps even given her an opportunity to escape.

"You lying little bitch! You've gotta know where it is. You're the only one she could've told. I'll get it out of you before—'' He made a grab for Willow, but she veered backward. The seat of the chair brushed the back of her legs and she inched around it, her terrified gaze locked with his as he stalked her across the room.

An image of torture surfaced in her mind once more. Willow wanted to retract her denial, to say she was lying about the money, that it was buried in her backyard. But her vocal cords were paralyzed again, and she could only continue to move backward until she felt a sudden warmth along her left side. Though she guessed she was near the kerosene lamp on the orange crate, she kept her glance fixed unwaveringly on Frank Fielding.

The exultant gleam in his eyes told her he meant to drive her into a corner, then pounce on her like a rabid animal. She was determined not to let him get that close. Guided by the primordial instinct of survival, she whirled suddenly, snatched up the kerosene lamp and flung it at him.

The sound of breaking glass as the lamp shattered on the floor drowned out Fielding's startled gasp. Instantaneously flames burst on the front of his jacket. He beat at them furiously, the only light in the room the glow from the tongues of fire that licked hungrily at his coat.

Willow scurried around him in the hindering darkness, shards of glass crunching under her shoes as she felt her way toward the door. She had gone only a few feet before she careened into the chair. The loud crash it made when it hit the floor blended with Frank Fielding's mingled cries of pain and fury. The instant she gained the freedom of the outdoors, she made a dash for his car.

She couldn't remember whether Fielding had told her to take the keys out of the ignition or whether he had removed them himself. She ran around to the driver's side, jerked open the door and sent up a prayer of thanksgiving when she found them there. In the fraction of a heartbeat, she slid under the wheel, her shaking fingers turning the key. She heard the jumbled sounds of shouts and curses issuing from the cabin, but paid them no attention.

The engine sparked to life, sputtered, then died. Willow tried again and again, and every time the engine caught, gave a sickly sputter and died. ''Damn! Please, God! Please!'' she beseeched. When her prayer went unanswered, she frantically pumped the gas pedal and kept on pumping it as she turned the key. A sob of frustration ripped from her lips when a couple of moments later she smelled gasoline and knew she had flooded the engine.

Hysteria seized Willow by the throat. She wondered frenziedly what to do. She was wasting time; the precious seconds of her life were ticking away with alarming speed. She had no idea if Fielding was hurt badly or not. She knew only that he might come charging after her at any minute, that she had to get away. But how?

She chose to take her chances on the road, the only way of escape available. She was dreadfully aware that she would be exposed, a running target on the open track, but she refused to let that dissuade her. She opened the car door and started to get out, only to slam it shut again when she heard a sudden noise nearby. Willow snapped her head around to see Fielding silhouetted in the doorway of the shack. A bright glow threw him into bold relief; the fire had spread to the hut.

He started toward the sedan, murderous rage bristling in every inch of his stocky frame.

With a whimpering sob, Willow swiftly locked the doors. Even though there was no one around to hear, she screamed and leaned on the horn. He began to strike the window on the driver's side with his fists. Failing to break the glass, he gave an enraged bellow and bent down and groped along the ground. Willow tried to start the car again, but the engine was still flooded.

At that moment Fielding stood up and attacked the window with a large rock. Each blow struck a death knell in her ears. She screamed again when she heard a sharp splintering sound. Minute cracks were spreading upward from the center of the window.

Suddenly a shaft of headlights pierced the darkness. Through the pounding inside her head Willow could hear a car engine. A vehicle was traveling toward the cabin, apparently at high speed, because she caught only a brief flash of it on the road before it vanished to swing around the shack.

It crossed her mind that Frank Fielding had an accomplice, the owner of the hut perhaps, since Fielding presumably lived near the California prison where he worked. The possibility that he wasn't alone in his kidnapping plot congealed the blood in Willow's veins. But then she saw Fielding's look of surprise. He paused in his attempt to shatter the car window. He whipped around as the other vehicle came to a screeching stop a few feet behind the gray sedan.

Shocked incredulity widened Willow's gray eyes. She blinked, sure for a moment that what she saw was a figment of her imagination created by fear and hysteria. Steven had sprung from his Jaguar and he was rushing at the prison guard.

"Oh, thank God!" The tidal wave of relief that swept over her after the terror-laden tension of her ordeal left her weak and giddy. She surrendered to the sobs of pent-up emotion wrenching her body.

When she looked up again, she saw Fielding racing toward the road, with Steven in hot pursuit. Steven caught him with a flying tackle that sent him sprawling facedown on the ground. The two men rolled over and over, their bodies locked in fierce combat. Then Steven was straddling Fielding and raining brutal blows on his fleshy face.

From inside the car, Willow heard the grinding sound of bone against bone as Steven struck the other man. Each blow in itself was enough to knock him out, but Fielding managed to slither out from beneath Steven. In a second he had shot to his feet and begun to run for the road. Steven caught him again, and spinning him around, dealt him a right cross to the jaw, following with an upper cut. Frank Fielding fell heavily to the ground and was still.

With the realization that he was no longer a threat to her, Willow leaped from the sedan and flew into Steven's open arms. His breath stirred her hair, and his rapid heartbeat thudded against her breast as he held her tightly to him.

"Are you all right? He didn't hurt you, did he?" Steven held her slightly away from him, his eyes scanning her features in the gloomy light. But she was trembling so badly, her teeth chattering so fiercely, that she could only nod.

To still the tremors that shook her with the warmth of his own body, Steven gathered her close once more. Willow nestled against him, not quite able to grasp the fact that she was safe at last. She wanted to remain in the sheltering circle of his arms forever. But he released her after a moment and went to stand over the inert body of the prison guard.

"Who is this bastard? Why did he bring you to this godforsaken place?"

"H-his name's F-Frank Fielding. He's a guard at the prison where Cassie w-was." Willow cleared her throat and took a deep breath to steady her quavering voice. "He kidnapped me to find out if I knew where the money from the robbery was. He was going to kill me because I could identify him." She shuddered at the awareness of how close she had come to death.

"My God! Well, he won't get a chance to hurt you or anybody else for a long time, if ever. Let's get him to the police and report this fire while we're at it."

Willow glanced over her shoulder to see flames darting up the outside walls of the hut. When she turned back to Steven, she saw that he had taken off his belt. He rolled the unconscious Fielding onto his side and used the belt to bind the man's hands behind him. For the first time Willow noticed that the guard had shed his coat and speculated that it had spread the blaze to the tinder-dry shack.

"We'll leave his car here. The police can get it later, if the fire doesn't get it before then. We'll have a tight squeeze in the Jag with all three of us, but we can make it. I want to keep an eye on this bird, so you'll have to drive, I'm afraid. You okay? Think you can handle it?"

The Jaguar had a standard shift. Although she hadn't driven with a standard shift since high school, Willow felt sure that she could manage well enough. She nodded. Together she and Steven dragged Fielding to the car and stuffed him into the cramped back seat. Steven got in next to him.

The cabin, now fully engulfed in flames, burned like a beacon in the darkness as Willow drove away.

Since she was sadly out of practice, she ground the gears at first. The car lurched and bumped along the dirt track before she finally got the hang of handling it. She had been so shaken until then that she hadn't given any thought to how Steven had known to come to the shack. She asked him now.

"I didn't. I heard someone honking a horn and drove in that direction. I went into the rest room while I was waiting for you at the bar. When I came out, I looked out the window to see if I could spot you and saw this bastard forcing you into his car. I recognized it as the same sedan that followed us the other night. So I went after you, but lost you shortly after you turned onto the first dirt road. I drove around blindly until— Well, you know the rest." Steven ended on a note of self-disgust, angry with himself for having lost sight of the gray sedan.

Willow thanked God that she had honked the horn when she had, that Steven had looked out the bar

window at precisely the right moment. If he hadn't...
She refused to let her mind finish the half-formed
thought. She looked into the rearview mirror when
Fielding began to moan, indicating that he was re-
gaining consciousness. It was so dark that Willow
couldn't see anything, and felt rather than saw him
struggle.

"That won't do you any good. You've got an appointment with the police, and I'm here to make sure
you keep it. So just cool it or I'll give you more of
what you got back there." Steven's warning was a
promise rather than a threat. The ominous quality of
his terse tone left no doubt but that it was a promise
he wouldn't hesitate to keep. The prison guard immediately ceased to struggle.

As the sheriff's office in Carson City was the nearest law enforcement agency, Willow drove in that
direction when she turned onto the highway. Steven
and their prisoner were silent for several minutes.
Then the latter remarked, his speech slurred as if he
were groggy, his voice stiff, apparently from his sore
jaw, "Why'd you have to stick your nose in this? It
was between me and her. I probably wouldn't have
done much more to her than rough her up some, anyway."

"That's not the way it looked from where I was.
And you can bet I'll say so to the cops! Keep your
lying mouth shut till then. The sound of your voice
offends me. I'm liable to knock you around again just
for the hell of it!" Steven's tone was as brutal as his
fists. Neither man spoke after that, and Willow concentrated on her driving until they reached the sheriff's office a few blocks east of the courthouse.

Steven marched Fielding into the sheriff's office, Willow trailing them. They came into a small room that had a counter running the width of it. A blond woman deputy looked up as they entered. Steven positioned himself between Willow and Fielding, and Willow was glad. She wanted Fielding as far away from her as possible. Taking command of the situation, Steven explained why they were there, and told the deputy about the fire. She in turn called the nearby fire department, then summoned a detective who came out to talk to them.

When Willow had reported the abduction, the policeman, who introduced himself as Detective Jacobs, told her, "Since no officer was present when you took him into custody, I'll need to have you make a citizen's arrest." He moved around to the other side of the counter, slid a form across to Willow and supplied her with a pen.

While she was filling in the necessary information, Fielding complained, his raspy voice surly, "Do I have to stand around here and listen to this crap? My hands hurt like hell, and I'm feeling lousy all over. I need to see a doctor. Will you get whatever I'm tied with off, for God's sake?"

"Somebody really did a number on you, by the look of you." The middle-aged detective's unsympathetic glance traveled over the prison guard's battered face and the angry crimson burn that covered his throat.

"They sure as hell did! She tried to roast me, and this bimbo almost beat me to death with his fists!"

"After what you tried to do to her, you're lucky I didn't finish the job, you sniveling son of a bitch!" Steven rounded on Fielding, his face purple with fury, but Detective Jacobs stepped between the two of them. He removed the belt from Fielding's wrists. His hands were raw.

"Looks like second-degree burns," Jacobs observed dispassionately. "We'll have somebody get you to the hospital. Then you'll have some questions to answer."

At his signal, the woman deputy summoned two officers, who took Fielding into custody. They handcuffed him and moved him out the door for the ride to the hospital. After he and his two jailers had disappeared from sight, Detective Jacobs led Willow and Steven to a room in the rear of the building to interview them.

When she was relating Fielding's reason for having abducted her, Jacobs interrupted to say, "I remember the robbery. It caused quite a stir around here. But why did he think you knew anything about the money?"

"Because I was Cassandra Clayton's best friend, and I was the last person she saw before she died. He thought she'd told me where the money was. He didn't believe me when I said she hadn't." Willow shivered, recalling the deadly intent in Fielding's eyes just before she had hurled the kerosene lamp at him. She also remembered having felt, on the day of Cassie's memorial service, that something that would touch her own life had begun. She wondered if that feeling had been a forewarning of tonight's occurrence.

Jacobs asked, "Is that why you think he was going to kill you?"

"I don't think, I know. But that's not why. He was going to murder me because I accidentally saw his face when we were struggling. He knew I could identify him," Willow replied, suddenly irritated. She was mentally and physically exhausted, her ravaged nerves stretched to snapping point. She was angry, too, about the harassment she'd been subjected to because of the missing money first by Addison Clayton, then by Brad, now by Fielding. She wondered if it would do any good to take out a full-page advertisement in all the newspapers disclaiming all knowledge of it.

"Sorry. Bad choice of words," the detective apologized. He asked her just a few more questions before he turned to Steven.

Steven's information was brief and to the point. As Willow listened, she tried to regain her emotional equilibrium, but she began to shake once more when he described Fielding's smashing the car window with a rock to get at her. Steven reached out to give her fingers a gentle squeeze.

"Miss Laughlin's been through hell tonight. I'd like to take her home as soon as possible."

"Sure." The older man smiled to signal his understanding. "I'll need you both to make out a statement, and you'll be called to testify at Fielding's trial. Meantime, relax a minute while I go get the statement forms."

After what seemed an eternity, the two were finally told that they could leave. With a supportive arm around her waist, Steven led Willow to the Jaguar and helped her inside. Only then she remembered that she had left her Camaro at the bar and had dropped her evening bag during her frantic attempt to outrun Fielding. Her keys were in the bag, as well.

Steven said, "I'll go back later for your car, and if I can't find your purse, I'll get a locksmith to change the locks or make you a new set of keys. You've got an extra house key, haven't you?"

Willow told him she kept a spare key in a wind chime near the door.

"Good. Don't worry about that now. Just close your eyes and rest."

Willow obeyed gladly, aware all at once of the pounding headache she had developed. Absently she brushed her fingers across her forehead and discovered a goose egg the size of a fifty-cent piece. It must have been made when Fielding had forced her into his car. Still, all things considered, she supposed she was extraordinarily fortunate in not having sustained anything more serious during her terrifying ordeal. With that thought, she leaned back and concentrated on releasing the tension in her body in the hope that it would ease her headache.

Steven turned the car around and headed toward Willow's house, his mind on the kidnapping. On the occasion when Fielding had followed them, the incident had left a sour taste in his mouth. Now he knew why. His thoughts flashed to the unadulterated terror he'd seen on Willow's face when he'd shot past the sedan in pursuit of Fielding. Most women would have been reduced to a mindless mass of hysteria when confronted with the same situation, but from what Willow had told the detective, she'd fought Fielding tooth and claw and had even had the presence of mind to throw a kerosene lamp at him. Steven had known from the beginning that she had plenty of spunk, and now she had proved what a little dynamo she really was.

There was something more important to think about than Willow's actions against Fielding, though: her statement to the police, especially one particular portion of it. Steven's reflections revolved around that until he swung the Jaguar into Willow's driveway.

Trixie curled up beside Willow on the sofa when Steven made her sit down.

"What you need is a good stiff brandy. It'll put the starch back into you and calm your nerves. I could do with one myself, come to think of it. Hang on, I'll be back in a flash," he tossed over his shoulder as he went into the kitchen.

He returned momentarily with two snifters of brandy and sank down beside Willow. His hair was tousled, his face bruised and streaked with dirt, his impeccably tailored dark blue suit grimy, all the result of his skirmish with Fielding.

Despite the warming effect of the brandy, Willow felt chilled to the bone. She shivered again, and Steven quickly set his glass down on the coffee table. "I should have taken you straight to the hospital instead of bringing you home. Had them give you a tranquilizer or something. You're obviously still in shock." He set her snifter aside as he spoke and, holding her to him, brushed a whisper-soft kiss over her injured forehead.

Willow drew comfort and strength from his gentle embrace. She had always detested hospitals, found them intensely depressing places with their clinical atmosphere and cheerless decor. As for tranquilizers, she'd taken them only once in her life and hadn't cared for the drug hangover she had had afterward. She told Steven that both were unnecessary. At his doubtful look she added, "I'll be fine in a while, really. I think I'll just take a long hot bath. That should take the chill away and help as much as any sedative."

When Steven remained unconvinced, Willow made for the bathroom. Steven relented but insisted on running her bath water himself.

"While you're in the tub, I'll rustle us up something to eat. That should make you feel better, too."

Willow was reminded of the dinner show they had missed. It seemed a lifetime ago that she had set out to meet Steven, but in reality only several hours had elapsed since then. Collecting her warmest nightgown and a fleecy robe, she glimpsed herself in the mirror of her bedroom bureau and was appalled by her appearance. Her lovely black-satin-and-lace dress was heavily creased, the right shoulder torn during her fierce struggle with Fielding. The goose egg on her forehead had already begun to turn purple; by morning she would be sporting an ugly bruise.

When Willow returned to the bathroom there was no sign of Steven, but he had switched on the overhead heater and liberally splashed bubble bath into the water. She smiled, touched by his thoughtfulness, as she undressed and stepped into the tub.

She eased her chilled body down until only her dark head was visible. The hot foamy water sluiced over her, a soothing balm, which almost instantly began to restore her emotional well-being. Her eyes scanned the beige-and-blue serenity of the familiar surroundings with mingled fondness and wonder. Only a short while before, she had been fighting violently for her life, yet here she was in the peaceful sanctuary of her home, with Steven nearby and Fielding safely in police custody.

It occurred to Willow to wonder if Fielding had made the obscene phone call, if he had been the prowler in her backyard and if he'd been responsible for having searched her suitcase. She couldn't imagine how he might have managed to go through her suitcase and didn't think he would readily admit to any of these things. Still, she couldn't help but wonder.

There was his trial to be faced, something that she quite naturally wasn't looking forward to. Indeed, the thought of having to see him again caused a knot of dread to form in the pit of her stomach. But with luck she wouldn't have to worry about that for weeks, perhaps even months. Until then she determined to do her level best to put the horrors of this night behind her, to derive satisfaction from the knowledge that the danger had passed and that Frank Fielding would never again be a threat to her or anyone else.

Chapter Ten

Willow emerged from the bathroom twenty minutes later to find Steven standing at the kitchen range. He turned at her entrance, still worried about her. "Are you feeling better now?"

"Yes, thanks. But it looks like you've been busy." Willow glanced at the assorted pots, pans and bowls that littered the countertop and wondered curiously what he had been cooking. Judging from the array of utensils, he had prepared enough food for at least six people. No fruits of his labor were visible; he must have put whatever it was into the oven. He had combed his hair and washed the dust from his face. There was something else about him, which brought an amused grin to her lips.

Steven was wearing a frilly blue apron over his dark pants. Oddly enough, the apron increased rather than diminished his masculinity, but he obviously didn't think so. A tinge of scarlet stole up from the collar of his white shirt as he met Willow's amused look. "I couldn't find anything else to cover my pants, and none of your terry-cloth dish towels would fit around my waist. Don't you have anything to cook in that doesn't have ruffles?''

"Uh-uh. Besides, you look cute, and that baby blue really brings out the dark highlights in your hair." Willow stepped up to him and planted a playful peck on the tip of his nose.

Steven suffered her teasing but whipped off the apron as quickly as he could and laid it across the counter. He turned back to her with a lopsided grin that contained a mixture of embarrassment and relief. "Well, at least I'm glad to see that your run-in with that bastard Fielding hasn't hurt your sense of humor any. We'd better eat what I've fixed before it gets dry. You sit down and I'll bring it to the table."

As Willow sat down, Trixie turned away from her dish, licking her lips. Willow had given her a meal before she'd started out to meet Steven, but after his thoughtful gesture, she didn't have the heart to tell him that. Trixie looked as if she might burst at any moment.

Steven joined Willow presently, bearing a tray with plates of omelets, green salad and rolls. "Would you like coffee or milk?" he asked, setting the tray down in the center of the table. Willow chose milk, and when she started to get up, he said, "I'll get it. You start eating."

When Steven had mentioned food earlier, Willow had felt sure she wouldn't be able to swallow one bite. Surprisingly, though, her normally healthy appetite asserted itself, and she tucked into the light meal with more relish than she had expected. The omelet, which contained ham and cheese, was fluffy, the salad crisp, the rolls crunchy. Willow complimented Steven on his culinary efforts, and he remarked with another lop-sided grin, which she found enormously endearing, "Not all single men are fumble-fingered jerks in the kitchen, I'll have you know. I can throw something decent together when I have to, even if I do make a hell of a mess while I'm at it." He cast a rueful glance at the littered countertop.

They ate in silence for a while. Then Steven asked, his tone serious now, "Do you feel up to discussing what happened tonight? Sometimes when you've been through a trauma like this, it helps to talk about it."

"I suppose in some cases that's true. But I've decided to put the whole thing out of my mind and try to forget it. Thanks just the same." Willow reached out and squeezed his lean brown fingers to let him know how touched she was by his caring attitude.

"I think that's the best way to handle it." He returned the pressure of her fingers, his eyes warm with approval. "I don't think you should be left on your own, though, at least for tonight. I'll bunk in the spare room, if that's all right with you."

Though Willow hadn't paused to consider the night ahead, she realized that she had unconsciously been dreading the thought of being alone. She accepted Steven's offer with a grateful smile.

"I'll be leaving for work from here in the morning, so I have to stop by my place to pick up some things tonight. How about you? Think you'll feel up to going to work tomorrow?"

"I don't see any reason why I shouldn't. I'll probably look like heck with this thing—" she ran a finger over her swollen forehead "—but I don't feel bad enough to stay home." Actually she was feeling much better now that she'd eaten, and the food, combined with the aspirin she had taken in the bathroom, served to curb her painful headache.

"Good girl. I'm glad you aren't going to let this kidnapping thing get you down," Steven commended her. "When I go to my place to get my things, I think I'll ask Eileen to come and keep you company. I'll get your car while I'm out and see if I can get Mike to drive it back here."

Willow approved of asking Mike to drive her Camaro from the bar, but felt it unnecessary to have Eileen stay with her. "That's really sweet of you. I appreciate the suggestion. But I'm sure I'll be safe enough. I'll make sure the doors and windows are locked and leave all the lights on, too. Besides, Frank Fielding is in custody, and it's not as though you'll be gone long."

"I know, but I think it's a good idea, anyway. I checked with the sheriff's office while you were in the tub, by the way. They're keeping Fielding in the hospital overnight to treat his burns—under heavy security, naturally. Then in the morning he'll be behind bars where he belongs. Right now, why don't you go into the living room and watch TV or something while I tackle this mess. Then I'll give Mike and Eileen a call. Is their number in there?" He gestured at a small address book on a table under the phone.

Willow protested against Steven's doing the dishes by himself; for one thing, she knew where everything went. Far more important, she liked being with him. But he overruled her objections and shooed her out of the kitchen.

Left to her own devices, she listened to Steven moving around in the kitchen and the soft murmur of his voice when he spoke on the telephone.

"Mike and Eileen should be here anytime," he told Willow when he returned to the living room a few minutes later. On cue the doorbell chimed, and he went to answer it. Steven led the couple into the living room, but the instant Eileen spotted Willow, she rushed to her and seized her hands as she sat down beside her on the sofa.

"My God, honey! Steven said you were kidnapped by some creep from that prison Cassie Clayton was in. Are you all right? He didn't, er, molest you or anything, did he?" Eileen's hazel eyes expressed the shocked horror in her voice.

Willow quickly reassured her friend that Fielding had not sexually attacked her. Swallowing past a lump of revulsion that rose abruptly in her throat, she shook her head. "He had other things on his mind, thank heaven. I've never been so scared in all my life, and for a while I was sure I'd never see tomorrow. But yes, I'm fine." For a brief instant Willow relived the terrifying moment when she had spied the ski-masked figure with a knife in its hand. Determinedly she rejected the image and turned to Mike as he spoke.

"Well, that's something to be thankful for. But it looks like he banged you around some." His shocked expression matched Eileen's as his tawny eyes took in the goose egg on Willow's forehead. "Steve says the cops have the rat. I hope they toss him in jail and throw away the key. It must've been hell for you. Steve said he brought you right home from the sheriff's office, but maybe you should have a doctor check you over. Make sure you don't have a concussion or something. That's a pretty nasty bump you've got there."

To banish the troubled frown on Mike's brow, Willow assured him that she hadn't experienced the nausea or dizziness that generally accompanies a concussion.

Steven had stood quietly by while she talked to Mike and Eileen, but now he broke in to say, "I don't want to leave her for too long, so the sooner we get started, the better. That is, if you're ready, Mike?"

"Sure thing. You two sit tight. We'll be back as soon as we can. You keep an eye on our little gal," Mike admonished Eileen. "Make sure she's really okay."

As Steven went to the entry hall closet for his coat, Willow rose to make certain all the windows were locked. Anticipating her intention, Steven waved her back. With Mike's help he examined each and every one before they left.

No sooner had the front door shut behind them than Eileen turned to Willow. "Can I get you anything? Maybe an ice bag for your poor head? Mike's right—that is a nasty bump. Does it hurt much?"

"Some, but by morning most of the soreness and swelling should be gone. I don't think I need an ice bag, thanks. I feel like an invalid just sitting here. I could make some coffee, if you like."

"I came over to take care of you, remember? Thanks, anyway." Although a remnant of shock lingered on Eileen's face, her voice contained a quizzical note as she remarked, "You said that creep from the prison kidnapped you for some other reason than rape. What did you mean by that?''

Willow groaned inwardly when she glimpsed the inquisitive gleam in Eileen's eyes. She had told Steven she preferred not to talk about her terrifying experience, and her sentiments hadn't changed. But she knew her neighbor's curious streak well enough to know that Eileen would probably lie awake puzzling over possibilities if she didn't clarify her statement. She was aware as well that despite her curiosity Eileen was genuinely concerned for her welfare. Nonetheless it was with great reluctance that Willow explained, ''He knew I visited Cassie every chance I got and he thought she'd told me where the money from the robbery was.''

''But how did he know where to find you? How did he even know what town you live in?''

''He's the one who sent me the dollhouse, so he had my address. Steven and I spotted him a few nights ago when we went dancing. I guess he must have been following me around.'' The speculation that Fielding had been stalking her without her knowledge caused a creepy sensation to crawl up her back like a snake.

''Well, I suppose that was a natural conclusion. His thinking you might know something about the money, I mean. You were the last person who saw Cassie before she died, after all. And you said even her father had questioned you about it.''

Willow quickly latched on to Eileen's first remark. ''Maybe it is to you, but it isn't to me. Frankly, I'm sick and tired of being bugged about that damned money. Whose side are you on, anyway?'' she countered, suddenly defensive and angry once more. She was trembling again, too, and near tears, perhaps because of her friend's insensitive attitude, perhaps in reaction to her horrible experience. She might have gone on being angry had she not noticed Eileen's stricken look.

"Oh, God, sweetie. I didn't mean that the way it sounded. I'm on your side, of course, silly. Who else's would I be on? I guess I was just thinking out loud...." Eileen lapsed into chagrined silence. Then in a clear attempt to lighten the heavy tension, she remarked on a brighter note, "That Steven is something else. The way he came charging in to rescue you in the nick of time. He told Mike about it on the phone. He reminds me of a hero in a novel. I'm a real pushover for that kind of macho stuff, and I'll bet it made points with you, huh?"

Eileen's obvious efforts made Willow feel guilty about her irritated outburst. Eileen had willingly interrupted her evening to stay with her, had generously offered to do anything she could to ease any discomfort Willow might have. And now she had repaid her kindness by railing at her like a short-tempered shrew.

Feeling as if she were the most ungrateful witch alive, Willow swiftly apologized. Then in reference to Eileen's comments about Steven agreed, "He sure did. You should have seen the way he took out after Fielding and had him tied up almost before the brute knew what hit him." A proprietary smile crossed her face as she related the details of the short-lived fight, Steven's take-charge attitude at the police station and his solicitous attitude toward her since he had brought her home.

Afterward to make further amends for her angry outburst, she insisted on making Eileen some coffee. They were still sipping it when Steven and Mike returned.

"Your car's safely in the driveway, and I think this is yours?" Mike set her black sequined evening bag on the coffee table, and she asked how he had gotten hold of it. "Somebody found it in the street and turned it in to the bartender. Say, that java sure looks good. Got any more?"

When everyone had had enough coffee, Willow thanked Mike for getting her car and Eileen for having stayed with her, and Steven expressed his gratitude, as well. "Hey, that's what friends are for," Mike retorted, encompassing them both with a toothy grin. To Willow he said, "We're sure glad you're okay, kid. If you need anything else, just give us a holler. Only make it loud. This one snores." He helped Eileen to her feet and gave her rump a playful swat as he followed her out the door.

Steven accompanied them outside, and when he returned he had a hanger of his clothing slung over one shoulder and in his hand a slender black case containing films from his video library. "I thought you might want to watch some old movies to unwind." He set the case by the VCR, hung the clothes in the entry hall closet, then joined her on the sofa.

Willow couldn't help but be touched by his considerate gesture. At the moment, however, she had something more on her mind than viewing vintage movies. Wordlessly, she turned, and framing Steven's face with her hands, drew him to her for a long, deep kiss. She savored the tangy taste of his mouth slowly, fiercely, almost desperately, acutely aware of how close she had come to having been denied the pleasure of him, the instantaneous delight the feel of his mouth always awakened in her.

She went on kissing him with her lips, her soul, the very essence of her being. When at last she released him, she murmured, her voice quavery, "I forgot to thank you for saving me."

"Hmm. Well, have at it, lady. You couldn't have picked a nicer way." Before Willow could react, his mouth had swooped down on hers. Whereas her kiss had been desperate, his was gentle, filled with infinite tenderness, as if she were delicate crystal he feared might break at his slightest touch. Willow had a sudden urge to cry. Steven's face was a misty blur when he lifted his dark head.

He gazed at her in silence. Willow gazed back at him, her heart fluttering as he took her hand in his, studied it a moment, then carried it to his lips. With exquisite slowness he kissed each of her fingers. Willow stared at him transfixed, her throat constricting when he turned her hand over and began to kiss her palm. His touch percolated through her blood, and she gasped in surprise as his tongue darted out to trace a provocative pattern along her sensitized skin.

When Steven finally drew his mouth from her hand, he looked at her for another long, heart-stopping moment before pulling her into his lap. He kissed her again, this kiss deep, demanding, intense. Willow slid her hands inside his jacket and wrapped her fingers around his waist, the clean male scent of him pervading her senses. Longing and warmth stole over her, and her lips parted eagerly beneath his to welcome the probing shaft of his tongue. The force of his arousal sent a ripple of excitement through her. She reveled in Steven's nearness and the jackhammer trip of his heart against her breast.

Her long fleecy robe had slipped up over her legs, and she quivered as he stroked the silken flesh of her bare thigh. Then his hand reached upward to push the lapels of her robe aside. His fingers crept inside her nightgown and captured her nipples, massaging and coaxing the tips to stiff peaks. His lips traveled down the same trail, and the erotic invasion of his moist tongue caused Willow to whimper as if she were in pain.

She dug her hands in his hair and dragged him closer, the caress of his mouth on her breast creating so strong an urgency in her that she became lost in a labyrinth of desire. One part of her, the cautious part, warned her that she was entering dangerous territory, but her spiraling desire rendered her incapable of heeding the warning.

Steven's hand moved to explore the secret region of her femininity, and at the same instant something warm and wriggly launched itself at Willow's feet. She groaned in anguish. Trixie's timing could not have been more inappropriate, yet Willow could not ignore the animal's presence.

Trixie was looking at her with wounded eyes, and Willow sat up, her fingers trembling from unslaked passion as she reached down to pet the dog.

"I think our little friend is jealous," Steven observed. Rising, he stood with his back to Willow, removed his jacket, and carefully tucked his shirttail into the waistband of his trousers. A ragged quality underlying his amusement, a telltale jerkiness in his movements, gave evidence of his own unfulfilled desire.

With slow deliberation he folded his suit coat and laid it neatly over the back of the rocker. The smooth resonance of his voice when he turned back to her testified to the fact that he had regained complete control of himself. "You didn't say anything about the movies I brought. Want to see some or would you rather watch the tube?"

Willow marveled at his recuperative powers; she was still so shaken that she felt as if a minuscule whirlwind was whipping around inside her body. She took a steadying breath before she replied. "The movies, definitely. Let's see what you've got."

After the shocks and intense emotions of the evening, Willow wanted to watch something light and entertaining. Anticipating her mood, Steven had brought classic comedies and whimsical musicals. *Gigi* struck her fancy. Steven loaded the videotape into her VCR before rejoining her on the sofa.

Although Willow had seen the movie before, she thoroughly enjoyed viewing it again, cradled against Steven, her head snuggled against his shoulder. Wrapped in the warm cocoon of his arms, she felt secure and protected, so much so that she found it difficult to recall how suspicious of him she had been when they'd first met. The doubts that had driven her to find out if he'd lied about his job now seemed ridiculous. She trusted him implicitly, knew instinctively that she was right to do so. He had boldly rushed to her defense and saved her life, so how could she repay him with anything less than complete trust?

Willow stifled a prodigious yawn, suddenly so drowsy that she could hardly stay awake. As if her eyelids were weighted down by sandbags, they fluttered shut and despite her efforts to open them, they refused to budge. She burrowed more deeply into Steven's shoulder and surrendered to the drowsy feeling.

Steven lifted her in his arms and carried her into her bedroom. As he placed her gently on the counterpane, her eyes opened momentarily and she smiled. Then, with a little sigh, she turned over onto her side and slept once more.

Steven covered her with her blankets. Her cheeks were flushed, the sweet smile that curved her lips one of serene contentment. He'd had his share of women, had taken freely what they had offered without a second thought. But Willow was different.

For one thing, she roused protective instincts in him he hadn't known he possessed. Then, too, he had discovered very much to his surprise that he really liked her as a person; he admired her zest for life, her sense of humor, her indomitable spirit. Steven had reacted to her on a physical level from the beginning, and that hadn't changed. Hell, even now he wanted her so badly that he felt as if somebody had attacked his guts with a red-hot branding iron. But responding to her emotionally was something he hadn't counted on, and he wasn't sure he liked it.

Steven had been convinced he would get a better handle on things by putting some space between Willow and himself. He had lied to her about his nonexistent Utah trip so that he could focus his energy solely on what he had to do. Until tonight he had firmly believed that he'd succeeded. Now he wasn't so sure. He wasn't certain of anything, except that he was going to have to rethink this whole damned situation and probably approach it from an entirely different angle. But from which one? What track did you take when you'd been so damned sure you'd been following the right one all along?

The question loomed in Steven's mind as he watched Willow, a deep frown furrowing his forehead. Then, with a weary sigh, he strode into the spare bedroom, where he restlessly prowled the floor, his brain a tangled mass of confusion.

Chapter Eleven

The pale fingers of dawn spreading across the ceiling of Willow's bedroom bore faint traces of pink that heralded the coming sunlight. Willow stretched luxuriously, her body refreshed by the uninterrupted hours of sleep she'd had, thanks to Steven's reassuring presence.

She doubted that she would have closed her eyes all night if he hadn't offered to stay. She felt certain that in spite of her determination to put the terrifying kidnapping out of her mind she would have been a nervous wreck, starting at shadows, her heart leaping at every unidentified sound.

Willow thought about Steven's timely rescue, his tenderness, his gentle solicitude. Except for the love her parents had lavished on her when she was growing up, she'd never felt so cared for, so pampered. He had a way of making her feel more special than any man she'd ever known, more intensely aware of her femininity than she had ever been. Nor had any man's kisses possessed the power to send her desire soaring to such heights, not even those of the attorney with whom she'd been in love. But when it came to the art of kissing, Steven was a master, the attorney a mere novice. All this, coupled with her genuine regard for Steven, made for a powerful combination.

The raucous jangle of Willow's alarm clock intruded on her reflections, and afraid it would disturb Steven, she quickly turned it off. She assumed from the slumberous silence that drifted toward her from the spare bedroom down the hall that he was still asleep, and moved about quietly as she got dressed for work.

Although the swelling on her forehead had subsided, she did indeed sport an ugly bruise that no amount of makeup could conceal. Having applied two layers, she simply fluffed her hair over the injured area and let it go at that. The door to the spare bedroom was closed when she tiptoed past, but to Willow's surprise, she found Steven sitting at the kitchen table reading the morning newspaper, a mug of coffee in front of him. He was dressed in tan slacks and a brown turtleneck sweater; his dark hair was damp.

He spied Willow and glanced up from the paper with a smile. "Hi! I hope you don't mind, but I helped myself to your shower and borrowed your razor. I forgot mine last night. You're looking great this morning. Did you sleep okay?"

Steven was taking in the ultrafeminine lilac suit she wore with a pink ruffled blouse. His eyes were brimming with male appreciation, and she wasn't sure if he was commenting on her health or her appearance.

"Like a log. How about you?" Willow asked. She poured herself some coffee and carried it to the table.

"Uh-huh," Steven grunted, deliberately lowering his head so that Willow wouldn't see the blurriness in his eyes from the scant amount of sleep he'd had. In truth he had paced the floor until three, his thoughts having made him too restless to relax. The hell of it was, his nocturnal prowlings had proved to be a total waste of time; he was still as confused as he had been the night before.

Willow apparently didn't notice anything out of the ordinary, because she went on smiling at him, the sensual curve of her lips too inviting to resist. Steven leaned across the table and covered her mouth with a scintillating kiss that set his blood pounding in his veins, easing some of his tiredness.

"Umm, nice. To what do I owe the pleasure of that?" Willow murmured, her cheeks aglow from the warmth radiating through her.

"Pure provocation." Steven treated her to the lop-sided grin she was coming to adore. It faded and he grew serious as he sat down again. "There's an article about the kidnapping in here." He tapped the newspaper. "I'm even mentioned, but they spelled my name wrong. According to this, the cabin was completely burned, but the fire department got there before the flames did any damage to the surrounding area. Want to read it?"

"Thanks, but I think I'll pass," Willow said, suddenly annoyed. She had never liked the public exposure she'd been subjected to because of Cassie's involvement in the robbery, and this morning she liked it even less.

"Sorry, I guess that was a stupid question." Steven gave her an apologetic look and lit a cigarette.

"No, it's okay. It's only that after Cassie died, I thought things would simmer down and life would go on the way it always had. I'm beginning to wonder if that's ever going to happen.''

''I'm sure it will,'' he reassured her. Willow hoped he was right and that publicity of her abduction would be confined to the one newspaper; but the latter hope proved to be futile.

No sooner had Steven left for work and she had stepped outside on her way to the courthouse than she was met by a reporter she recognized as belonging to a TV station in Reno. Disconcerted color stained Willow's face as he started across the lawn toward her. Her sentiments about discussing the abduction hadn't changed, but she saw no way out, short of refusal, which she realized would make her appear rude and uncooperative. Feeling like a trapped animal, she watched as the reporter and his minicamera and crew converged on her.

The reporter shot questions at her so rapidly that she scarcely had time to respond to one before he threw another at her. By the time the interview was finished, Willow was rattled, embarrassed and even more irritated than before. It wasn't until she arrived at the courthouse that her annoyance finally began to lessen.

In the downstairs corridor she encountered some of her fellow employees, all of whom had evidently read the morning paper. Shocked sympathy was expressed, queries made, and Willow spent several minutes supplying the answers. She knew that, unlike the aggressive television reporter, her co-workers were inquiring out of concern. She kept that in mind when shortly after she had reached her office the telephone on her desk rang.

"Willow?" Brad Clayton identified himself. Then he explained, "I tried getting you at home, but got no answer. So I thought I'd try you there. Are you all right? I heard on the news a while ago something about you being kidnapped last night. I only caught the tail end of the report, so I didn't get all the details. Who was it? What did they want with you, anyway?"

Beginning to feel like a broken record, Willow assured Brad that except for the minor injury to her forehead, she was fine. "It was Frank Fielding, one of the guards from the prison Cassie was in. He was after the money from the armored-car robbery and thought I knew something about it because of my relationship to Cassie."

"Oh, God," Brad groaned as he digested the information. "The name doesn't ring a bell. I don't know if I ever knew him. But that must have been terrible. I'm so sorry about the way you've been hounded because of that damned money. I'm sure you think I'm as bad as everyone else after the way I went on about it the last time I saw you. I can't say I blame you and I'm sorry about that, too. But I meant it when I said I was attracted to you, which is another reason I'm calling. I'd really like to see you again, and I was hoping we could arrange something for tonight. Do you think that's possible?"

Brad sounded sincere, and Willow couldn't help but feel flattered. Still, for several reasons she decided to turn him down. Foremost, of course, was Steven. Willow was certain that she was in love with him. Then, too, she had always held steadfastly to the rule of dating only one man at a time. It prevented misunderstanding and saved a great deal of hassle, as well. Besides these reasons, she doubted that she would have agreed to see Brad, anyway. Although she had always liked him, she had never cared for the way he allowed Addison to dominate his life. She preferred strong, independent men who refused to walk in anyone's shadow. Like Steven.

Naturally she couldn't hurt Brad by giving him this assessment of his character, so she told him that she was seeing Steven exclusively these days. To spare his feelings further, she added, "If it weren't for that..." letting her voice trail away on a regretful note.

"Oh." Brad grew quiet as well, his silence fraught with disappointment. Then he said, "Say, come to think of it, the news report I heard mentioned something about Randall. He wasn't involved in the kidnapping scheme, was he? I remember last time I saw you, you seemed to think there was something funny about him. Made me so curious I decided to check on him, but I came up with nothing."

Willow conceded the point and assured him that her doubts had long since been allayed. "Steven's name was connected with what happened last night because he saved me from Fielding. If it wasn't for him, I wouldn't be talking to you right now." As Willow gave Brad a brief account of the prison guard's attempt to kill her, she shivered, seeing in her mind's eye the murderous expression on Fielding's face when he had stalked her across the cabin floor.

"Well, I'm glad Randall was there for you, even if I'd rather it had been me. The important thing is that you're okay. But if things don't pan out with him, give me a call," Brad urged, his voice still laced with disappointment.

"I will," Willow agreed, knowing that she never would.

ONCE THE NEWS of Willow's abduction had faded from the headlines, life resumed a normal pattern. Willow continued to see Steven almost every evening, and their time together became so special that she treasured each meeting as one treasures a rare and precious jewel. Things at work went so smoothly as well that there wasn't the slightest ripple to disturb the stream of days flowing gently by.

Then, as if to make up for her happiness, all hell broke loose, and Willow became a victim of Murphy's Law. Whatever could go wrong did.

A week after the kidnapping on a Friday morning, Willow overslept and was late for work; she and Steven had treated Eileen and Mike to a night on the town, then partied with them at their place until the small hours. Then her stenograph machine broke down during a court session of a criminal trial, and she was forced to delay the proceedings by rushing to her office for a replacement. The visiting judge, an irascible man, made a further delay by pulling her into his borrowed chambers and giving her a stern lecture on pride in professional conduct, which he considered Willow lacked. Afterward she slunk back into the courtroom, angry, humiliated and red-faced. But more was to come. During her midmorning break she chipped a tooth on a corn nut and had to make an emergency visit to her dentist during her lunch hour. In keeping with her monumental bad luck that day, she had to wait because she didn't have an appointment. Her only stroke of good fortune was that the afternoon court session had been canceled to allow the prosecuting attorney time to study additional evidence he had gathered against the defendant. So though it was after two, Willow decided to go home, where she would be able to unwind somewhat before returning to her office to transcribe her notes from the morning.

Since the dentist's office was only a stone's throw from the courthouse, she had walked there. Now, as she traced her steps toward home, she tried to forget the frustrations of the disastrous morning, no easy feat. She did the trick by recollecting a funny joke Mike had told the evening before and she was still grinning with amusement when she entered the house.

It wasn't until Willow had laid her coat and purse on the living-room sofa that she realized Trixie hadn't rushed to greet her as she normally did. There was no sign of her, in fact. Thinking that perhaps Trixie was curled up in her bed asleep, Willow called out to her.

"Well, now, that's odd," she mumbled when the dog failed to appear. "Trixie?" she called again. She began to wonder if her pet was ill. She made a thorough search of the spare bedroom and the bathroom but couldn't find her.

Increasingly concerned, Willow strode into the kitchen, her mind so absorbed with the dog that at first she didn't notice anything out of the ordinary. Then she stopped short just inside the doorway, a look of surprise replacing her worried frown.

The Victorian dollhouse lay in the middle of the floor. Willow stared at it in bewilderment, the dog abruptly forgotten, and wondered how on earth it had gotten there. In the next instant enlightenment dawned, and an eerie sense of uneasiness encompassed Willow as she realized that someone must have been in the house while she was gone.

Why somebody would have put the dollhouse on the kitchen floor was beyond her comprehension, but she didn't stop to consider the reason. She guessed from the pervasive silence that the burglar was gone and hurried to the phone to report the break-in to the police.

The receiver poised in her hand, Willow started to dial the number, only to hesitate when she heard a faint sound from somewhere nearby. Her ears strained to identify the origin of the sound. It came again briefly—Trixie whimpering. Willow slammed down the phone and hurried to the utility closet in the corner. Whoever had broken in must have put the dog in the closet to get her out of the way.

Her uneasiness supplanted instantaneously by anger, Willow threw open the closet door, her eyes scanning the floor. She spied Trixie, a huddled white heap, and started to console her. But the words died on her lips and prickly needles of fear stabbed at her scalp as she saw a flicker of movement in the shadowy recesses of the closet.

The pungent scent of menace suddenly permeated the air. Willow's senses shouted a warning, and obeying the dictates of her instincts, she turned and darted for the back door, her heart racing as fiercely as her feet. She heard a sudden surge of movement behind her and a frightened cry from Trixie.

Her fear-rigid fingers wrestling with the suddenly slick knob, she yanked open the door and launched herself outside, to be halted in mid-step by something dark, slender and cold, which slid down her face and was tightened around her neck by a powerful force from behind. Willow's air supply was abruptly choked off, her shriek of terror a feeble gurgle.

She coughed, sputtered and gagged, her hands flying up instinctively to pluck at the strangling noose, her feet automatically striking out behind to kick her unseen tormentor. She heard a sharp grunt as she connected with her attacker's shin. Willow threw herself back against a solid mass of muscle and bone, trying to thrust her fingers under the thing that was crushing her windpipe. But the garrote was tightened even more with a savage ferocity that made it dig deep into her flesh. She was being dragged back into the kitchen.

Willow's eyes started to bulge, her oxygen-starved lungs screamed for air and her senses began to reel. Skyrockets burst in a fiery shower of color through her head, and the room slowly began to recede around her. The knowledge that someone was deliberately choking her to death pierced her terror-bludgeoned brain, and Willow struggled violently in a final attempt to save herself.

To no avail. Blackness descended on her like the impenetrable folds of an obsidian curtain. She heard a muffled rapping sound that reverberated in her spinning head. Consciousness slipped away, and she knew no more.

Chapter Twelve

Willow drifted, her body weightless, ethereal, a feather floating on oceanic waters. Only she wasn't on water, she was in the stygian void of space, somewhere between heaven and hell. The word *purgatory* penetrated her torpid brain; she had always wondered what purgatory was like, and now she knew. It was cold, frightening, painful. She hurt all over. Most of the pain seemed to be around her neck. She tried to swallow, but the pain grew so intense that she felt as if someone had shoved broken glass down her throat. She groaned and with the effort began to drift once more.

She had no idea how long she continued in her weightless drift. There was no sense of time in these spanless reaches between death and eternity, only the awful pain, utter darkness and a dreadful loneliness such as Willow had never known before.

Suddenly she heard her name called and realized that she wasn't alone in purgatory after all. Someone else was there as well, someone whose clutching hands on her shoulders wrenched her back to earth with a bone-jarring jolt, which wrung another groan from her.

The knowledge that she was alive and breathing followed, and momentarily came the memory of the violent attack made on her. It occurred to Willow with a sudden surge of stark terror that her unknown assailant had remained to finish the murderous business. The thought ripped through the clinging tendrils of unconsciousness and brought her to complete awareness. Ignoring the waves of nausea that rolled over her, she struck out blindly to ward off another attack, her flailing arms so heavy that she could scarcely lift them.

"Willow!" the voice called again, this time with an unmistakable urgency that communicated itself to her and caused her to cease struggling. She opened her eyes, but her head was spinning so fiercely that she saw only a shapeless blur, and her ears were ringing so loudly that she couldn't tell if the voice was that of a man or a woman. When her vision slowly began to clear, the shapeless blur solidified and became the features of someone she recognized. She was so stunned that it took some seconds for her befuddled mind to identify the features of Eileen. But what was Eileen doing here? And where was here, anyway?

Willow turned her head and discovered that she was in her own kitchen. She became aware of the hard surface of the floor beneath her pain-riddled body, of the back door standing open. A bright ribbon of sunlight streaming through the doorway hurt her eyes, and she closed them to blot out the searing pain. When she opened them again, she noted the naked anxiety on Eileen's face, her ashen color.

"My God, honey!" Eileen said unsteadily. "I thought you were dead!"

Willow wanted to say she had thought so as well, but she was so dazed and her throat ached so abominably that she was incapable of speech. She could only look up at Eileen and be grateful that she was alive.

Eileen said, her tone laced with shock, "When I found you, that thing was wrapped around your neck." With revulsion, she pointed to a brown extension cord a foot or so away from where Willow lay. Willow shivered convulsively. A shudder slammed through her with the force of a savagely wielded fist, and she knew from the incredulous horror on Eileen's face that she had guessed what the cord had been used for. She was glad Eileen didn't put her thoughts into words, because they would have hurtled her over the brink of control and plunged her into a pit of hysteria.

As the violent tremors shook Willow's body, Eileen rose and quickly closed the back door. "I called for help and somebody should be here any minute. You stay here where you are while I run and find a blanket to cover you."

Eileen started out of the kitchen, tossing the remark over her shoulder, but Willow croaked, the intense pain in her throat causing her to grimace, "No...please... I don't...want to stay here...." The cheery kitchen was repugnant to her after the terrifying violence of the assault. She couldn't wait to escape from the room. She saw Trixie huddled under the table, still frightened by having been shut in the util-

ity closet, and gave her a consoling look as she struggled gingerly to a sitting position.

Eileen saw her and swiftly returned to her side. She
looked doubtful. "Gee, honey, I don't know if you
should be moved or not. They always say when a person's been in a car accident or something not to move
the victim." Willow was tempted to remind her that
she was not the victim of an automobile accident, but
she didn't feel like speaking any more at the moment.
Besides, she was too busy fighting off a fierce onslaught of dizziness from the effort of sitting up.

There was no need for her to speak. Sensing Willow's determination, Eileen bent down, and putting
her arm around Willow's waist, helped her gently to
her feet. Another wave of dizziness enveloped her, this
one so sharp that the room began to recede once more.
Willow thought she was going to faint for an instant
and closed her eyes again until the giddy feeling
passed.

"Are you all right?" Eileen's arms tightened around
Willow's waist. Willow nodded, and Eileen said,
"Okay, let's take it easy now, one step at a time."
They moved together slowly, Willow's gait so un-
steady that she felt as if she were an infant just learn-
ing to walk. They had gained only a few feet when she
noted something that brought them to an abrupt halt.

The dollhouse lay on the floor. She stared down at
it as though it were some foreign object she had never
seen before. She wondered confusedly what it was
doing there, then recalled having found it when she
had searched the house for Trixie. She was about to
ask Eileen to put the dollhouse back in the dining
room, but reading her mind, Eileen said, "I think we'd

better leave it where it is, at least until the police get here.''

Eileen was right. Willow nodded, and they proceeded into the living room.

After what seemed an endless journey, Eileen eased Willow down onto the sofa, then covered her with a blanket from the linen closet in the hall. Willow was still trembling so furiously that her teeth rattled; her body was chilled to the bone. She gathered the blanket around her, seeking warmth from its woolen folds.

Just then the earsplitting shriek of a siren rent the air. Eileen hurried to the door. Willow heard a murmur of voices and Eileen returned with three firemen, who brought with them rescue equipment. One of the firemen, a balding man with glasses, whose jacket insignia identified him as the captain, came over to Willow.

"Feeling kind of rocky right about now, hmm?" He smiled down at her and she nodded. "Well, let's have a look at you, see how you're doing." He knelt beside her, placed both hands on the side of her neck and with gentle fingers carefully but expertly examined her throat. He spent several long, agonizing moments probing the area around her Adam's apple and painstakingly scrutinizing it. Despite his gentle touch, his exploring fingers tortured Willow's throat, and she winced in protest.

"I know, it hurts like blazes." He gave her a commiserating smile. "But I've got to make sure everything's intact. Now let's see if you can talk. Your friend—" he gestured toward Eileen, who stood at the edge of the scene along with the other two firemen

"—tells me somebody took an extension cord to you. Was it someone you know?"

"No. At least…I don't think so…." Willow's voice was so raspy that she hardly recognized it as her own, her throat so raw that it felt as it had when she'd had her tonsils removed at the age of five.

The captain smiled as though pleased that she could speak. He signaled for one of the other firemen to give him a canvas bag. From this he removed a stethoscope, pushed the blankets down around Willow's waist and listened to her heart. At the same time Willow heard the front door open. Soon the two deputies who had investigated the prowling incident entered the room.

"A little fast, but normal, under the circumstances," the captain pronounced with a nod at the officers, who followed Eileen to a quiet corner of the room. "There's a pretty nasty welt around your neck, but otherwise you seem to be fine. Wouldn't hurt any, though, to spend a few hours in the hospital for observation."

As on the night of the kidnapping, Willow disdained the idea of going to the hospital. "It's up to you." The captain shrugged, his expression doubtful. "Just keep warm and eat soft foods for a day or so for that sore throat. You'll need to sign a patient refusal form, too."

Willow signed the form, scarcely recognizing the shaky scrawl as her own customarily neat script. She lay back and watched while the two firemen removed their equipment. The captain spoke to the police officers briefly; then he departed, as well.

A moment later the two deputies approached with Eileen, who held Trixie in her arms. The dog struggled to be set down. Eileen released her and she jumped up beside Willow, nestling against her for reassurance.

"Sorry to bother you. I know you must be feeling pretty rotten, but we need to know what happened," the more slender of the two deputies said. Willow recalled vaguely that his name was Walters.

Even though some of the dizziness she'd experienced when she first regained consciousness had diminished, she was indeed feeling rotten. Still, she realized the importance of relating the details of the attack so that the police could find the person responsible.

She told him she understood. But Eileen broke in to say, her glance darting from one officer to the other, "If you're finished with me, I'd like to go. I'm not feeling real great myself." To Willow she explained, "I took off from work early because my ulcer kicked up. Too much spicy stuff last night, I guess," she said in reference to the Mexican food to which Steven had treated her, Mike and Willow. "Right now it feels like I've got a raging wildfire in my stomach."

Eileen had never mentioned an ulcer, and the news came as a surprise to Willow. It hadn't occurred to her to wonder what Eileen was doing there, but Eileen explained, "I saw you pass my place a while ago and came over to borrow some antacid. I knocked on the door, then when you didn't answer, I came on in."

Willow recalled the muffled rapping sound she'd heard in the instant before she had passed out; it must have been Eileen knocking. Though she was sorry Eileen had an ulcer, she was profoundly grateful for her providential visit, for she realized it was this that had scared off her attacker. And from the lingering horror in Eileen's face, she knew her friend realized this, too.

Willow reached out to clutch Eileen's hands. They clung together for several silent, emotion-packed seconds. "I...I'm sorry. I don't use antacids...but thank you for..." Her hoarse voice trailed away, and another convulsive shudder ripped through her body.

"Try not to think about it. I'll have Mike pick up some Maalox on his way home from work. Speaking of that, shall I call the courthouse and tell them you won't be back today? Shall I see if I can get hold of Steven?"

Returning to work was out of the question, so Willow considered Eileen's suggestion about contacting Steven. Except for when she had phoned the realty company to verify his employment, she'd never bothered him at work. She was reluctant to do so now. But she longed for his gentle strength, needed to draw comfort from him as she had done on the night of the kidnapping. She assented to both suggestions.

Eileen made the calls, then said, "Steven isn't in his office right now. They're going to try and find him, so you should be hearing from him before too long. I'm glad you're going to be okay, honey. I'll give you a buzz later to see how you're doing."

As the front door closed behind Eileen, the officers turned to Willow. The stocky one, Deputy Haggerty, as Willow remembered, waited with pen and notepad to take down the necessary information.

A million cobwebs seemed to have attached themselves to her brain. She took a deep breath to clear her mind, her hand absently stroking Trixie as she mentally sorted through the details of the attack. When she had them in chronological order, she told her story to the policemen. She deduced now that whoever had attacked her must have heard her enter the house, hidden in the utility closet and pulled Trixie inside to keep the dog from giving away the hiding place.

Officer Haggerty glanced up inquiringly from his notepad. Anticipating what he was about to ask, Willow said, "I couldn't see who it was. Everything happened so fast, and it was . . . it was kind of dark in the utility closet. . . ."

Her mind flashed back to the moment when she knew with blood-curdling certainty that she was going to die. She felt again the murderous grip of the extension cord around her throat, crushing her windpipe, strangling the life out of her by horrifying degrees. Tremors seized her slender body, and she closed her eyes, fighting to control her emotions.

Understanding her distress, Deputy Walters reassured her, "It's okay. It's over and you're going to be just fine." To Haggerty he remarked, "Sounds like a burglary attempt." The other officer agreed, then turned back to Willow. "Did you notice anything missing when you were looking for the dog?"

Despite her efforts to blot it out of her mind, the memory of the attack remained so strong that Willow couldn't think clearly. She paused, considering the question, then shook her head. "No, but I didn't realize then that somebody had broken in."

"We'd better check the premises out. We'll need your help for that. Feel up to looking things over?" Deputy Haggerty asked.

Willow was still feeling so rotten that she didn't want to speak anymore, let alone move about. But she realized the necessity of searching the house to find out if anything had been taken. She rose reluctantly from the sofa and accompanied the two officers as they examined all six rooms. Not wanting to be alone, Trixie padded after them. Nothing seemed to be missing, nor was there any sign of forced entry. It was impossible to tell how the intruder had gained access to the house. Only the dollhouse seemed to have been disturbed, a fact that struck Willow as decidedly strange.

Deputy Walters voiced Willow's thoughts. "Whoever got in was evidently only after the dollhouse. But you came in, preventing the theft. I'd even venture to say he or she probably used the extention cord as a means of putting you out of commission so they could escape."

In spite of the murderous strength with which the cord had been applied, Willow was inclined to agree with his theory, simply because there was no earthly reason for anyone to want to kill her. She watched silently as, with the aid of dish towels, Deputy Walters picked up the extension cord and the dollhouse and set them on the counter. He called the sheriff's office for a fingerprinting unit, and while he was still on the phone, Deputy Haggerty escorted Willow back into the living room, where she sank down gratefully on the sofa, her legs weak from the mild exertion of walking.

His pencil poised to write, he asked, "Do you know why someone would want to steal the dollhouse? Is it valuable?"

"I don't really know. I guess it must be worth about four or five hundred dollars, but it's certainly not valuable. And no, I have no idea why anybody would want to steal it." Willow's tone reflected the mystified expression on her face. "In fact, it doesn't make any sense. I—" She paused, suddenly wondering if, since the dollhouse had come from Cassie, someone thought it was somehow linked to the armored-car robbery. Perhaps the intruder even thought the dollhouse contained the money itself. This was impossible, of course; there was nowhere to conceal two million dollars in the little building. Soon Willow recalled having found the dollhouse turned sideways, the double doors at the rear open. At the time she had thought she had done it herself while dusting, but guessed now that somebody must have gotten in and tampered with it.

"Taylor's on his way," Deputy Walters said to Haggerty, rejoining them in the living room.

"Good." Deputy Haggerty gave him a cursory glance before turning back to Willow. "You stopped as if you'd thought of something. What was it?"

Willow told him of her belief that the dollhouse had been tampered with, adding, "It was a gift from Cassandra Clayton. She and I were close friends, and I'm wondering if maybe someone thinks the dollhouse has some connection to the robbery she was involved in."

"I remember the case. Everybody in the state heard about it because of the Clayton name. Caused quite a scandal. Never could figure out myself why such a rich girl would do something like that." He shook his head, still perplexed by Cassie's participation in the crime in spite of all the months that had passed since then. "Do you think the dollhouse *could* contain a clue about the money?"

"No. Cassie never talked about it or the robbery, and I've always believed she didn't know anything about the money," Willow was quick to reply.

"How can you be so sure it doesn't?" Deputy Walters countered just as swiftly. "Better check it out," he muttered to the other deputy. At their insistence Willow followed them back into the kitchen. She stood quietly by, a look of incredulity on her face as both officers carefully examined each room of the dollhouse without touching anything.

When they stepped back moments later, Deputy Walters removed his visored cap and scratched his head in confusion. "It would help if we had some idea what we were looking for. Are you sure Miss Clayton never said anything that might indicate there was a clue in the dollhouse?"

"Cassie didn't know the whereabouts of the money, so she could hardly have planted any clues. She sent me a letter with the dollhouse, but I'm sure it has nothing to do with any of this."

"Maybe," Deputy Walters conceded. "Just the same, let's have a look at it, anyway."

Although Willow was convinced that the letter would yield nothing, she led the way into the dining room with the officers trailing closely behind. She pulled open the drawer in which she kept the letter along with her good stationery and other writing materials, but couldn't see it. Thinking she must have overlooked it, she went through the drawer again, without success.

"That's funny. It was here a couple of days ago," Willow muttered, recalling that she had seen the letter when she'd gone to the drawer for paper with which to drop her mother a line. Still, to make certain she hadn't put it in another drawer, she searched the others thoroughly.

But the letter was gone, as though it had vanished into thin air.

Chapter Thirteen

"You're sure it was there?" Deputy Walters asked when he, Willow and Deputy Haggerty had returned again to the living room. The two officers remained standing, Willow resumed her seat on the sofa and Trixie curled up beside her once more.

Willow assured him that she was and why. He expressed the thought that by this time had occurred to her. "The intruder must have taken the letter. You say you don't believe either it or the dollhouse has any link to the robbery money, but it's pretty obvious that somebody does or they wouldn't have tried to get them. Do you remember what Miss Clayton said in the letter?"

Willow hadn't read the letter since the day she had received the dollhouse. As she was still fully convinced that neither could possibly contain anything relating to the money, she gave Walters' question only cursory thought. Now that she was becoming more alert, she was infinitely more concerned with who had gotten into the house and attacked her. "Cassie talked about the dollhouse, how she'd made most of the furniture herself, where she'd ordered the kit...."

Willow lapsed into silence as she pondered the all important who. Her mind automatically fastened on Frank Fielding. She told the two officers about Fielding's abduction of her, adding, "Do you know if he's still in jail?" Gingerly she touched her throat, which now felt like a gigantic bee sting because she had been talking so much.

Deputy Haggerty had been writing in his notepad, but stopped. "That's right, I remember hearing about it. He's out on bail. Got out a couple of days after his arrest. I know, because I was covering for one of the deputies who works in the jail and I processed this Fielding myself. Didn't his kidnap attempt have something to do with the money?"

"Yes...." Willow hesitated, the information about Fielding's release flooding her with uneasiness.

Deputy Walters reassured her, "We'll scout around and see if he's been spotted in the area since he got out." The doorbell chimed just then. "That's probably Taylor. I'll get it."

He returned with a small man who carried what Willow guessed was a fingerprinting kit. The three men went into the kitchen, and Willow heard the low hum of conversation as the little man went about his business. When this was completed he departed, and the two officers prepared to leave, as well.

Before doing so, Deputy Haggerty said, "We'll let you know if we turn anything up about Fielding and whether or not Taylor was able to get any fingerprints. We've made sure all the windows and the back door are secured. We'll get the front door on our way out. Get some rest, and try not to worry about Fielding. If he's anywhere in the vicinity, we'll nab him. Make no mistake about that.''

In spite of this promise, Willow couldn't help but be intensely uneasy about Fielding's release. He had to have been responsible for the theft of the letter, the attempt to steal the dollhouse and the vicious assault on her. He was the obvious suspect—except for two things, which only now occurred to her.

Willow had surmised that Fielding had tried to steal the dollhouse so that he could examine it for clues leading to the missing two million dollars. The same applied to the letter. But he'd had ample opportunity to study both before forwarding them to her. So why would he have tried to take them later?

Unless it wasn't Fielding.... Because Willow couldn't comprehend why he would want to take the dollhouse or the letter after all this time, she concentrated on those who also knew about the miniature Victorian house.

Steven, Eileen and Brad knew, and probably Addison, Mike and Jennifer, as well. Willow recalled Steven's interest in the dollhouse the first time he'd seen it, the way he had studied each and every floor so intently. She had set his unconcealed interest down to admiration of Cassie's fine craftsmanship then and still did. Also, since Steven seemed to have nothing to gain by trying to steal the dollhouse or the letter, she instantly rejected him as a suspect. Mike, too, for the same reason. Jennifer Clayton simply because she hadn't seen nor heard from her since Cassie's memorial service.

Brad, on the other hand, was an entirely different matter and not so easily dismissed. Granted, he had seemed genuinely upset when he apologized for the way she'd been harassed about the money. But he had made it abundantly clear on the day Willow had had cocktails with him how important it was to his family for the money to be recovered. He had stressed the significance of finding it in order to restore honor to the Clayton name. He had been pleading, almost desperate, which, in Willow's opinion, put him at the top of the list of suspects.

Nor was Addison exempt. Although Willow deemed him ruthless enough to resort to theft and assault, she didn't think he would stoop to doing his own dirty work; she reasoned that he would probably have left that to Brad. Yet if Brad had thought the dollhouse or the letter held clues that would reveal the whereabouts of the money, why not ask Willow's permission to examine them? She would have cooperated, regardless of her skepticism.

As for Eileen, Willow hadn't the remotest idea of what she would have to gain by attempting to take the dollhouse. Although her interest in it had been as keen as Steven's, surely that was because it had been a gift from Cassie. Eileen had always been remarkably curious about Cassie. But so what? That didn't cast suspicion on her any more than her inquisitiveness about Willow's relationship with Cassie.

The recollection of Eileen's curiosity coaxed a wan smile to Willow's lips. Then, suddenly, a recent remark of Eileen's rose unbidden to her mind and changed her smile to a frown. On the night of the kidnapping Eileen had considered Fielding's belief that Willow knew something about the money a natural conclusion. Willow recalled the annoyance she'd felt at

Eileen's insensitive attitude. It crossed her mind to wonder now, though, whether Fielding's erroneous assumption had seemed so natural to Eileen because she entertained the same notion.

Hot on the heels of this, other memories followed: Eileen's having been the only person Willow had told about the letter, Eileen's fascination with Cassie's excursion into crime, her avid interest in Willow's prison visits, her relentless questions about what she and Cassie had discussed during those visits.

Willow remembered, as well, the night she'd spied the prowler in her backyard. Eileen had phoned to say she hadn't come over because she had rollers in her hair and didn't want to be seen. Willow had found this excuse amusing, since having curlers in her hair hadn't prevented Eileen from appearing on the scene of a domestic squabble not long before. As for her ulcer, that had come as a surprise to Willow, because Eileen had never mentioned such a problem. They had shared any number of personal confidences since they had become friends, and now that Willow thought about it, Eileen's omission seemed odd.

She wasn't sure precisely where these recollections were leading, until all at once another unbidden thought surfaced: the third person in the armored-car robbery. That person's identity had never been discovered and, for all anyone knew, it could have been a female. Indeed, Cassie had participated in the crime, so why couldn't that unknown accomplice have been another woman? Eileen?

The prospect seemed too incredible, too fantastic, and Willow rejected it at first. But as if a dam had burst in her mind, questions surged forth out of control.

Had Eileen's curious inquiries about Willow's prison visits been a subtle way to elicit information about the money? Could Eileen have stayed away the evening of the prowling episode for fear that if Willow saw her so soon after the event she might have realized the prowler had been a woman? In regard to today's occurrence, aside from Steven, Eileen knew Willow's daily routine better than anyone. Could she have gotten into the house, thinking Willow would be at work, found and stolen the letter and tried to take the dollhouse, too? Then when Willow had come home later than usual, had she attacked her with the extension cord in fear of being identified? Afterward had she remained on the scene to play the role of innocent friend? Was borrowing medication for a previously unmentioned ulcer an excuse to explain her presence, the ulcer a trumped-up reason for being home on a workday?

Last but by no means least, Willow remembered Eileen's having rented the house next door shortly after Cassie's conviction. Although she hadn't thought anything about it then, she wondered if Eileen could have learned of her relationship with Cassie and become her next-door neighbor to cultivate a friendship in the hope that Willow would lead her to the money.

Willow closed her eyes, dizzy once more, not so much from the lingering shock of the attack but from the ideas that were spinning through her head. An image of Eileen swam through her swirling senses. She saw again the incredulous horror on Eileen's face during those moments when she'd first regained consciousness, horror that surely had been too real to have been feigned—unless Eileen was a consummate actress. Was she? Was Eileen in reality an evil deceiver, a she-wolf disguised in lamb's clothing?

Willow didn't know what to think or whom to suspect. She knew only that she felt drained from the aftermath of the assault and more afraid than she had ever been. Indeed, now that she was alone, the house had taken on a tomblike silence she found eerie, frightening, profoundly disturbing. When there came a knock on the door, she hurled herself to the floor as if she'd been fired from a cannon.

"Willow?" She heard the muted sound of Steven's voice and hastened to let him in. She caught a brief glimpse of his troubled look in the instant before she launched herself into his arms. Her "I'm so glad you're here" was muffled as she buried her head in his chest. Steven clasped her tightly to him; the buttons of his jacket bit into her cheek, but she hardly noticed. She pressed closer, deriving strength and intense comfort from his nearness.

Steven must have detected the raspiness in her voice. After some moments he held Willow at arm's length and snapped on the entry hall light so that he could see her more clearly. He looked worried.

"What's wrong with your voice?" he demanded, scrutinizing her sharply. Before she could reply, he spied the welt on her throat. "Good God! Your neck," he whispered, bundling Willow to him again. "Somebody left a message at the office while I was out saying to get here as soon as I could. What happened?"

In the enveloping shelter of his arms, Willow told him about her coming home later than usual and about the attack on her. Next she told him her speculations about the reason for the break-in, the attempt to steal the dollhouse, the actual theft of Cassie's letter. Steven listened, his face somber, drawn, whether from shock, anger or both she couldn't tell. When she had finished, he led her into the living room, sat down on the wing chair and pulled her gently into his lap.

"You said the thief apparently believes the dollhouse and Cassie's letter might contain information about the armored-car robbery money. The police think it's a possibility. What's your opinion?" Trixie left her place on the sofa to leap up on Willow's lap, but Steven kept his attention fixed on Willow.

"I think they're barking up the wrong tree." Willow's hoarse voice held the ring of conviction. "I've never thought Cassie knew where it was. I still don't." Even though the excitement had passed, Trixie seemed to be suffering the residual effects. Her little body was still quivering as if she were cold. Knowing exactly how she felt, Willow drew her closely against her.

Steven digested the information slowly, methodically sifting through the details Willow had imparted. The last part stuck in his mind like a needle in the groove of a phonograph record. Careful to keep his tone one of innocent curiosity, he commented, "I didn't know you'd gotten a letter with the dollhouse. You may not think they have anything to do with the money, but it's darned sure somebody does."

"I didn't bother to mention the letter because I didn't consider it important. Why—? Oh, Lord, don't tell me you think there could be something to that

malarkey about them holding some sort of clue, too?"
Willow slanted a cynical look at him.

"I don't know," Steven murmured noncommittally. "Who's to say there isn't? Could there be something in the letter and the dollhouse that could be construed as a clue? Maybe you'd need both to figure out what it is."

"Of course not. I've already told you I never thought Cassie knew where the money was. So how could there be?" Willow countered, wondering why he was so persistent. Still, someone had taken the letter and tried to steal the dollhouse, so she supposed his questions were natural enough, under the circumstances.

Aware of the harassed tinge in Willow's tone, Steven decided he'd better not press the point any further. He changed tack abruptly. "It's too bad you didn't get a look at whoever was hidden in that closet."

Willow was inclined to agree with him, but then she remembered that Fielding had tried to kill her because she'd identified him, and changed her opinion. Reminded of what the police had said about Fielding's release, she told Steven the news.

"The police said they'd check to see if he's been seen in the area and let me know. At first I felt sure he must have been the one who attacked me and I still believe it could have been him, even though he had the dollhouse and the letter before he sent them to me. But there are a couple of other people I'm wondering about, too."

Willow confided to Steven her suspicions of Brad and Eileen and her reasons for them and she told him her theory that Eileen could possibly have been the third accomplice in the armored-car robbery. Steven lapsed into introspective silence, his eyes narrowed, an intense frown crinkling his high forehead.

After another protracted pause he said, "I'll bet my Jag it's that bastard Fielding. His having access to the dollhouse and letter doesn't mean a thing, if you ask me. He could've thought he'd overlooked something and wanted another crack at 'em. I can't buy that bit about Eileen being involved in the robbery, either. Sorry, but it seems pretty farfetched. She strikes me as a very nice lady, without a dishonest bone in her body, the kind of teacher every kid wishes he had. She's vivacious and attractive. Some of the teachers I had were real dragons, as I remember."

Steven's voice was filled with undisguised admiration, and for a fleeting instant Willow experienced a sharp pang of jealousy. She dismissed it and challenged him, "But what about everything I've told you about her? All the questions she asked about Cassie? You think her fascination with Cassie was just harmless curiosity, those other things coincidences?" Despite the fact that she trusted Steven's judgment, she was only slightly persuaded. Although Eileen had been a good friend and it distressed Willow to imagine her capable of such wicked behavior, a shadow of doubt remained.

"As I said, I'd bet the Jag it's Fielding," Steven repeated with conviction. "If he is around here, he'd better hope the cops find him. Because if I get to him first, I'll wring his neck with my bare hands!" A savage fury settled over his face at this threat. Willow glanced away, suddenly discomfited, even though his

anger wasn't directed at her. Much as she feared
Fielding, she could almost feel sorry for him if indeed
he was still in the vicinity and Steven encountered him.

Aware of her discomfiture, Steven made a visible
effort to curb his emotions. When Willow glanced
back at him, she noted with relief that his face was
calm, and his voice was reassuring when he advised
her, "Try to put everything out of your mind. I'm here
and I'm not going anywhere. I'll spend the night here
again to make sure nothing else happens. I won't
bother going home for anything this time. I'm not
going to leave you even for a while."

Steven drew Willow close again to cover her lips
with his, and the tenderness of his touch banished the
last vestiges of her distress. She nuzzled against him,
enormously grateful that she wouldn't have to face the
coming night alone.

ONCE MORE Steven was gentle, solicitous, sensitive to
Willow's every need. At bedtime he even insisted on
tucking her in and murmured soothing words to her as
if she were a child afraid of the dark. But although his
protective presence shielded Willow from the outside
world and she felt quite safe, she could not relax. She
was restless, tense, tired to the point of total exhaustion, yet sleep eluded her long after Steven had gone
to his room. In spite of his advice to put everything out
of her mind, she thought about the attack, her suspicions of Eileen, Brad, her fear of Frank Fielding.

When at last she closed her eyes, dreams of the recent events stalked her in her uneasy slumber. In one
she was back in the ramshackle cabin to which Fielding had taken her, but the narrow cot was changed into

a torture rack to which she was lashed, and Fielding stood over her, tightening a mechanism that wrung shrieks of pain from her when she denied any knowledge of the missing money. Just when she was certain she could no longer endure the excruciating agony, the scene suddenly changed and she was in her own kitchen.

As if she were watching a movie, she saw herself fleeing to the back door to escape the person concealed in the utility closet. Once more she glimpsed the slender extension cord as it came down in front of her eyes, felt its brutal grip on her throat. Her assailant wore a long hooded robe rather than contemporary clothing, and where the face should have been, she saw a skull, which was grinning grotesquely.

The nightmare was so terrifyingly vivid that Willow woke with a cry, gasping for breath, her body drenched with perspiration. Her heart pounded against her ribs, and it took several moments for her beleaguered brain to register the fact that she was in her bed. In spite of her effort to go back to sleep, she lay for what seemed forever, peering into the encompassing darkness.

Finally, thinking a cup of hot cocoa might relax her, she gave a disgruntled sigh, snapped on the lamp and got up. Her body still felt hot and sticky, and without bothering to cover her thin chiffon nightgown with a robe, she stepped out into the hall. She wondered if her distressed cry had disturbed Steven, but she guessed from the heavy hush that issued from behind his closed door that he was sleeping.

In spite of her demand that he throw the extension cord into the trash, he had shoved it into a drawer in case the police needed it. He had put the dollhouse into the dining room. The kitchen bore no trace of the violence that had occurred there—at least, no visible trace, Willow thought, as she flicked on the light over the counter. She knew that a lingering sense of violation would prevail for a long time to come.

Thrusting the unsettling knowledge aside, she splashed milk into a saucepan and set it on the stove to warm. Though she had overcome the distress with which she had awakened from her nightmare, it had left a knot of tension in the back of her neck. Willow rotated her head to ease the tightness, but paused when she heard a faint rustling sound behind her. She turned to find Steven standing in the doorway, watching her.

Chapter Fourteen

Steven's chest was bare, his feet, as well; he was wearing only the gray slacks he'd had on earlier. He remained poised on the threshold, his gaze traveling slowly over her body and lingering over the slender curves of her thighs, the flat plane of her stomach, the upthrust breasts exposed to his view. Willow felt her body flush, not from embarrassment, but from the clinging warmth of his eyes, eyes that told her he very much liked what he saw.

The soft scraping of a rosebush against the window was the only sound in the room. Willow recalled she'd once wondered about the amount of hair he had on his chest. It was curly, dark, a shadowy triangle tapering down to his flat belly, just enough to enhance his masculinity. He advanced toward her, running his hand through his ruffled hair. "I thought I heard a noise and got up to see what it was. You okay? Is your throat hurting?"

"I'm sorry. I had a couple of really weird nightmares and couldn't go back to sleep. No, my throat isn't feeling too bad now." The pain in her throat had subsided to a dull ache, which was uncomfortable but

not unbearable. The salve Steven had found in the
medicine chest and applied to the welt had made it feel
better, as well. "I was just fixing myself a cup of hot
cocoa. Want some?" Willow absently rubbed the knot
of tension in her neck.

"No, thanks. But maybe this will help." Steven positioned himself behind her and gently massaged her
throat, his fingers carefully avoiding the injured area.
Willow closed her eyes and leaned against his chest, his
rippling muscles warm, solid, at her back. His touch
was delicate, light, yet highly effective. In a matter of
minutes she felt the knot disperse, the tension leave her
body.

She relaxed completely, but tensed again with
abrupt awareness when his fingers drifted down from
her neck to move in languid circles over her shoulder.
She felt the tickly sensation of his breath on the back
of her neck, the increasing warmth of it as he suddenly snared her earlobe between his teeth and began
to nibble the tender flesh.

Willow's breath became constricted, and her arms
moved upward to wrap themselves around his neck, a
tiny shiver rippling along her spine as he plunged his
tongue inside her ear. It traced a series of delicious
circles, which set her heart hammering wildly against
her ribs. Slowly Steven turned her around to draw the
soft curves of her body into the hard masculine contours of his own. Beneath the filmy folds of her
nightgown his hands caressed her slender hips, her
rounded buttocks, his touch for all its gentleness searing Willow's skin. Momentarily his hand began a slow,
provocative upward path. His eyes kindled. Cupping

her bare breast, he gently kneaded the burgeoning nipple.

Willow's gasp of shocked delight was muffled against his mouth as it came down on hers in a kiss so potent that her legs nearly buckled with sudden weakness. Her lips parted to receive his kiss, her fingers stealing up to bury themselves in his hair. Steven's breath was harsh, shallow; and, spurred to desire herself, she drove her tongue past the barrier of his teeth to taste the darkened interior of his mouth. It was moist, fresh, the musky male scent of him a powerful opiate that threatened to knock her senseless.

The milk was bubbling, but she ignored it. She returned Steven's demanding kisses with mounting ardor in the culmination of a sexual tension that had been building in them for weeks. Willow had struggled against her desire, determined not to rush headlong into another relationship. But she ached for Steven with a need such as she had never experienced. Only he could satisfy it.

When he raised his dark head, his eyes flashed the message of his own urgent need; he, too, realized the time for restraint had passed. Steven reached out to turn off the stove. He scooped her up into his arms. As if she were as light as thistledown, he carried her into her room and deposited her gently on the bed. He lay beside her and took her in his arms once more, his mouth claiming hers in kiss after heady kiss, their bodies close, their tastes merging.

At last his lips left hers, and his caressing fingers slid the thin straps of her nightgown over her creamy shoulders, past the fullness of her breasts, down to her waist. He lifted her slender hips fractionally to ease her out of the gown. By the lamplight, he studied her body as he would have studied a precious piece of art hidden away for centuries and exhibited for a once-in-a-lifetime view.

"Beautiful... I knew you would be," he murmured, his voice husky, his eyes dark with passion. Steven drew Willow against him once more, his hair-roughened chest grazing the tender flesh of her taut breasts. Of its own volition her hand reached up to stroke his face, but he caught it and guided it down to his chest. She caressed the hard surface, the touch of his bare skin causing her fingertips to tingle. He captured her stroking hand and cupped it over his stiff nipple. Silently Steven framed her head with his own hands and drew it down to his chest. Instinctively aware of what he wanted, Willow took the nipple between her lips and teased it with her tongue and teeth. A tremor went through him and she reveled in the effect her sensual ministrations were having on him.

Willow's lips explored every inch of Steven's chest. A fresh spark of passion ignited in her when he leaned her gently against the pillows, his possessive mouth covering her breasts, his tongue flicking out to coax the pink tips to a rigidity that produced a sudden ache far below. She dragged his mouth to her own and devoured him with her lips. But she wanted all of him. She moaned in protest when, as if to deny her that which she longed for most, Steven eased his body away from hers. Willow tried to draw him back, a question in her languorous eyes, but he eluded her with a sensual smile.

She watched, scarcely able to breathe, as he rose to remove what little clothing he had on. His bronzed body was lean and muscular, and Willow feasted her eyes on him, the ache inside her so fierce that it was almost pain. That sensual smile still curving his mouth, Steven lowered himself to her again. They explored their bodies until neither could endure the erotic torture a moment more.

With a ragged sigh Steven rolled over on Willow. His hands held her hips to take her, her thighs parted eagerly to receive him. Their bodies interlocked. They soared to lofty pinnacles of passion, then plummeted to the low-riding valleys of soul-shattering ecstasy. Together they willingly became lost in the ultimate communion of sharing, of offering and receiving, their bodies moving in a matched rhythm of pleasure as ancient as the earth itself.

Willow wanted desperately to capture and hold forever the sweet rapture that was filling her to the depths of her being, to nurture it, to prolong the inevitable conclusion of their long-awaited union. But she could not control the mounting pressure that was building in her and carrying her toward that unavoidable end. She felt a rushing sensation, an exquisite explosion. She cried out, her voice mingling with Steven's as he shuddered and gave a moan that seemed to come from the very core of him.

Lying in Steven's arms, Willow was cradled in a peace and contentment she'd never known. A delectable lassitude spread through her entire body. She smiled at Steven as he put his lips to her forehead and brushed back the moist tangle of her hair. She pressed her face into his neck, neither of them speaking nor moving. Willow had no words to describe what she was feeling in the aftermath of their rapturous lovemaking. She was too relaxed, too drowsy to speak, swept away on the wings of slumber, dark, gentle, comfortable. With a deep sigh of satisfaction, she closed her eyes and drifted off, her face still buried in Steven's neck.

Long after her measured breathing told him she was asleep, Steven held her in his arms. Then, so as not to disturb her, he laid her head down gently on the pillow, his eyes scanning her face. She was so beautiful that just looking at her made his heart swell. He'd known for some time that getting intimately involved with her would be a calculated risk, but after the kidnapping he had decided to take that risk, to savor the moment, and to hell with the possible ramifications of his actions.

He pondered those ramifications but drew only a blank for his efforts, so he turned his thoughts to action. He slid carefully from the bed, drew on his pants and on bare feet tiptoed quietly out of the room. He groped his way through the semidarkness to the kitchen, where he took a flashlight from a drawer. With the same silence and care, he stepped into the dining room, switching on the flashlight as he came to a stop in front of the maple hutch.

The beam of the flashlight flooding the dollhouse was brighter than he'd anticipated. There hadn't been time for more than a quick peek inside it when he'd put it away earlier. He studied it extensively now, the beam of the flashlight moving slowly over all three floors, lingering here and there as something caught his eye. But he saw nothing that even resembled a clue. The letter would have helped—if, in fact, it and the dollhouse did hold some hint that might lead to the money. Unfortunately the letter had escaped his hands.

A soft jingling sound behind made Steven stop abruptly. He turned, wondering how he was going to convince Willow that his secret search was founded on simple curiosity. Then he smiled sardonically when he saw that it was only the dog. The jingling sound he'd heard was made by her collar.

"You have the damnedest habit of turning up in the wrong place at the wrong time, don't you, you little devil? I would've thought you'd have learned a lesson after today," Steven muttered, suddenly irritated. Trixie wagged her tail as if he'd said something friendly. She padded after him when he returned the flashlight to the kitchen drawer and followed him into the bedroom. Steven slipped silently back under the blankets, noting with relief that Willow was still dead to the world.

EARLY MORNING SUNLIGHT trickled in through a chink in the curtains and settled on Steven's sleeping face. Willow propped herself up on her elbow, her eyes moving over the thick tousle of his hair, his aquiline nose, the dark stubble on his deep-cleft chin. The virile beauty of him filled her heart so that it brimmed to overflowing. Unable to resist the temptation, she stroked his cheek tenderly and brushed the disheveled strands of his hair away from his forehead.

Steven muttered an unintelligible sound, and a smile played across his mouth. His lids fluttered open, and his slumberous eyes looked into Willow's an instant before they traveled slowly over the satiny curve of her cheek, the creamy skin of her shoulders, the soft

mound of her breasts half-covered by the sheet. He
tugged the sheet away, exposing her naked body, and
she saw the film of sleep leave his eyes, the awakening
passion in their dark depths. He lifted his hand to
mold her rib cage and buried his head in the deep valley between her breasts, burrowing provocatively first
with his mouth, then with his tongue.

"I can't think of a more pleasant way to wake up."
The words were muffled against the swelling fullness
of Willow's flesh. His breath bathed her skin with a
delicious warmth, which was like a soft caress. Willow framed Steven's head with her hands to press him
to her, desire kindling in her as his mouth took hers in
a long, languid kiss. "You're almost too beautiful to
be real," he murmured thickly as he lifted her to lie on
top of him. She felt the solid length of his thighs, the
throbbing hardness of his desire as she melted into
him.

The tip of Willow's tongue traced the contours of
his lips before it plunged inside them, marking out
tantalizing circles, which elicited a low groan from
him. He matched her kiss for kiss, his masterful
tongue creating its own erotic path. Then he eased her
gently onto her back and trailed his hand over her
breasts, teasing, tempting, seducing, as he drifted his
way down to stroke the shadowy triangle of her femininity. His wondrous touch caused her body to set up
a thrumming vibration that sent delectable shudders
through her.

Willow arched against him, her fingers entangled in
his hair. A wordless plea gleamed in her eyes for him
to end the exquisite agony of wanting that was rapidly building in her, to cool the fever of passion rag-

ing in her body that threatened to reduce it to a burned-out cinder of longing.

Steven covered her with the length of him. Their bodies fused, becoming a single entity, one soul. Whereas he had made love to her the night before fervidly, now he loved her slowly, languorously, deliberately keeping his churning passion within rigid bounds until he had swept her over cresting waves of ecstasy and brought her to the blissful shores of sweet fulfillment.

They lay still, their bodies intertwined, their breath labored. After a while Steven settled Willow against his side, her leg lying against his hip. ''There's nothing I'd rather do than stay this way all day,'' he murmured, his voice a low rumble in her ear as she laid her cheek against his chest. ''But I've just had a great idea.''

''Whatever it is, it could never begin to top the one you already had.'' Willow grinned provocatively as she wound the hair on his chest around her fingers.

''Umm. Thanks. You really know how to stroke a guy's ego. It's Saturday, and since neither of us has to work, I thought we might go to my cabin in Lake Tahoe. We could spend the weekend there, if you haven't got any plans. I think it would do you a world of good to get away. You can relax, get your mind off what happened yesterday. You can bring Trixie, too, if you don't want to leave her alone that long.''

Steven had mentioned his cabin once before, but Willow had forgotten about it. She knew he was right. She did indeed need to get away, not that she could possibly ever forget the attack made on her. It would remain in her memory forever. But she didn't want to dwell on that now or think about Fielding, Brad and Eileen.

Contrary to her promise, Eileen hadn't called. Maybe she had guessed Willow suspected her and was purposely staying away. If she had actually been telling the truth about her ulcer, perhaps she hadn't felt well enough to phone. Willow knew that she was going to feel terribly guilty if Eileen was really ill. She considered telephoning her to ask how she was, but it was too early to call. Besides, if Eileen was lying, she would likely go on doing so.

"I think your idea is wonderful, Steven," Willow said, releasing herself reluctantly from his embrace. "I'll throw some things into a suitcase and be ready in no time. We can stop by your place for whatever you need on our way out of town."

"No need to. I keep extra clothes at the cabin. You'd better bring along your ski equipment, too, if you have any. I heard last night on the news the snow pack's just right for skiing."

AN HOUR AND A HALF LATER Steven halted the Jaguar beside a cabin nestled picturesquely in the pines on the south shore of Lake Tahoe. The bright sunlight glistened on the white-mantled ground and made the illusion of rainbow-shot prisms of multifaceted diamonds. Willow filled her lungs with the brisk pine-scented air as she emerged from the car. Trixie dashed past her straight for the nearest tree.

Steven collected the provisions they had stopped to buy when they reached the lake, Willow gathered up her suitcase, called Trixie and the three of them entered the cabin.

It was spacious enough to accommodate at least six people. The interior was rustic, but attractively furnished in earth tones. A large olive wood clock was hung on the wall. She recalled Steven's having said he enjoyed working with wood and guessed he had made it himself. He had mentioned he liked to paint, as well, but Willow saw no evidence of that. The cabin was almost as cold as the outdoors, and despite her heavy parka, Willow shivered and rubbed her chilled hands together.

Steven said, "It's freezing in here, I know. How about if you unpack the food while I go out and scare up some wood for a fire. That thing—" he gestured toward a wood-burning stove in a corner of the living room "—will have it cozy in here in no time. Then if you like, we can go skiing."

Willow approved. Having put away the groceries and left her suitcase in the largest of the cabin's four bedrooms, she returned to the kitchen for some newspaper with which to start the fire. Surprisingly enough, her own morning tabloid hadn't carried an account of the assault on her. Either it had escaped the notice of the press or it hadn't been considered newsworthy enough to report. Whatever the reason, she was glad. Reminding herself that she had come to the cabin to get away from everything involving the attack, she wadded up the newspaper and laid it in the stove so that it would be ready when Steven brought in the wood.

Having lived in snow country all of her life, Willow had naturally learned to ski. She had always considered herself fairly good at the sport, but soon discovered that she was no match for Steven. He soared over the slopes of nearby Squaw Valley as if his skis had sprouted wings. Whereas Willow tended to avoid the moguls, or bumps on the ski run made by other skiers, he glided over them with an expertise she envied. As if to impress her even more, he positioned himself on a high rock and jumped, landing about forty feet away. Then he flew down the face of a steep mountain at a breakneck speed that took Willow's breath away.

"Show-off!" she accused him, her heart still in her throat from his daredevil stunt, when she met him at the bottom minutes later, having plotted a much slower course down the mountain.

"Just thought I'd try my stuff." Steven grinned, obviously pleased with himself. He beamed even more proudly at the eloquent praises of other skiers who'd seen his dangerous antics.

In the evening, Steven treated Willow to a sedate but thoroughly romantic sleigh ride through the streets near the gambling casinos. In the night he made love to her again. Once more his lovemaking lifted her beyond the limits of anything she had ever experienced. She fell asleep cradled in his arms.

Over a late breakfast the next morning, Steven asked, "Would you rather lie around and be lazy today? Or would you like to get in some more time on the slopes?" A fleck of strawberry syrup from the waffles Willow had prepared dotted his mouth and he wiped it away with his napkin.

"Sounds good to me. As long as you don't think you're being featured on *Wide World of Sports* and scare the heck out of me like you did yesterday." Willow softened the retort with a smile as she gazed across the kitchen table at him.

"Well, you have to admit everybody else enjoyed it." Steven's grin was tinged with male pride.

"Everybody else doesn't l—"

Willow stopped short as what she had almost said sank in. She did love Steven, realized that she had loved him for weeks. This was the real thing, not a silly infatuation.

She was certain Steven felt the same way about her; his tenderness, his gentleness, his caring attitude emboldened her to think that very soon he would declare his love. Until then she would nurture hers, hold it gently to her like a cherished treasure. The recognition of her love for Steven brought a rare blush to her cheeks, a dreamy look to her eyes. She smiled, inwardly relishing the joyous feeling.

His eyes narrowing unconsciously, Steven's heart sank. There was no mistaking the love that glowed in Willow's face and that had almost spilled from her lips. When he'd decided to stop fighting his fierce desire for her, regardless of the consequences, he hadn't realized that one of them would be this. Instead of pleasing him, he found the discovery deeply disturbing and wondered how Willow would react if she learned the truth about him. A shadow crossed his face.

Aware of the heavy silence that had followed her slip, Willow said, "How about another waffle? I've been keeping a couple warm in the oven in case you wanted some more."

Steven ignored her question as if he hadn't heard it. He was scowling darkly, clearly lost in thought. His entire demeanor was brooding, aloof, as though he had abruptly retreated to some dark and distant place in his mind that she couldn't reach even if she tried. His remoteness produced a sudden chill in Willow, and she experienced a sensation of impending disaster so strong that she shivered involuntarily.

Only moments before, she had felt certain Steven returned her love, but all at once she wondered if she was wrong. Possibly there was something about their relationship that troubled him. Torn by her feeling of unease and her urgent need to know what was wrong, Willow reached out to cover his hand with her own. "Steven? Is something the matter?"

"I . . . What . . . ?" As if he had indeed been transported from some distant place and found the abrupt transition jarring, he stared at Willow uncomprehendingly. Then his expression cleared, and he fixed his attention on her. "Did you say something?"

"I asked if anything was wrong. You looked so remote, so preoccupied, I wondered if something was bothering you." Willow held her breath, her muscles tensing as she waited for his response. Still, if there was some facet of their relationship that troubled him, she would rather know about it now than find out about it later.

"I guess I've just got a lot on my mind," Steven hedged, unable to bring himself to tell her what he'd really been thinking about. He lit a cigarette and went into the living room for an ashtray.

Willow waited for him to explain what he had on his mind, but when he returned to the table, he merely said, "If we're going skiing, hadn't you better start getting ready? If you have any problem with zippers or snaps, just give me a yell. I'm great at that kind of thing.''

He gave Willow a grin filled with such male allure that it curled her toes. The awful sensation of impending disaster dissolved as if it had never existed. ''So I've noticed!'' she retorted with a sigh of intense relief.

They spent the late morning and afternoon on the slopes; Willow was extremely relieved that Steven didn't repeat his daring performance of the day before. Later they went for a long leisurely walk in the woods behind the cabin with Trixie. Then in the evening, they started back for Carson City.

To make the evening a festive one, Steven had stopped at a liquor store for a bottle of red wine. Now, back at Willow's house, they sat together on the sofa, enjoying the wine.

''You're such an expert skier,'' Willow remarked. ''Where'd you learn to handle yourself like that?'' Her voice held a mixture of admiration and envy.

''When I was a kid, my parents and I used to spend part of the winter in Colorado. My dad taught me the basics. The hotdogging I learned from a pro who worked at the lodge where we used to stay.'' Steven crossed one leg over the other as he spoke, smiling reminiscently at the memory, and balanced his glass of wine on his hip.

Tired of being ignored, Trixie, who had been lying unnoticed at their feet, suddenly jumped up between them. Willow shouted ''No, Trixie!'' But the warning came too late. The dog knocked Steven's glass from his hand, spilling the wine on his leg and onto the sofa.

Steven and Willow leaped up simultaneously, her exasperated "Oh, Trixie!" mingling with his "Whoops!" He pulled a handkerchief from the pocket of his tan cords and began to dab the wine stain, while Willow dashed into the kitchen for a dish towel. A mortified Trixie, tail between her legs, slunk into the bedroom.

Willow concentrated on the spot on Steven's cords, then on the ugly red smear on the sofa. It had spread to the cushion on which he'd been sitting. Steven had taken his wallet from his pants pocket and was rubbing it, the wine having soaked through to it.

"Here, let me do that." Steven held out the wallet, Willow reached out for it but missed. It fell on the floor, the contents spilling onto the carpet.

"Trixie's obviously not the only klutz in the family. Sorry," Willow apologized, stooping to pick up the papers, cards and currency.

"No problem." Together they collected the scattered contents of his wallet. Willow got up, only to bend down again to retrieve something that had slid under the coffee table.

"Missed one—" she began, but stopped suddenly as she glanced down at the object in her hand. It was a business card. Steven's, evidently. It had his name on it. Instead of identifying him as a real estate agent, however, it identified him as a private investigator with an office in Reno.

Chapter Fifteen

Willow stood still, shock and confusion on her face as she stared down at the card. She sensed rather than saw Steven rise, as well, but her attention was riveted to the card. She read it again carefully to make certain she wasn't mistaken and saw that she was not. Steven had been lying to her all along about his profession. Hadn't she suspected as much earlier, known intuitively that there was more to him than appeared on the surface? But why had he lied?

As if a light had been switched on in her mind, comprehension came. Recollection followed. Willow remembered that in several of their conversations Steven had steered the topic to Cassie. He was supposed to have been her friend, though Cassie herself had never mentioned him to Willow or evidently to her own family. On more than one occasion Steven had given her a probing stare, as if he sought the answer to some unspoken question. She thought she could hazard a guess now as to what that question had been.

Steven knew from Willow's stricken look what she was holding. Dammit! He'd been so sure he had removed all his business cards from his wallet. One of the things he had feared most was now bleak reality, and he knew he had better do some fast talking if he was going to redeem himself in her eyes. He opened his mouth, grim resignation on his features, groping for an explanation. Before he could say anything, she held the card out to him, her mouth set in a tight line, her voice stiff, unyielding.

"I think this is still usable." Willow scarcely recognized that frigid tone as her own. She was suddenly cold inside, too, with a deep chill that seemed to permeate her very bones. Even her soul felt as if it were frozen by the realization of Steven's deception.

He took the card, crumpled it and stuffed it into his pocket. "Willow, you've got to let me explain. I—"

"Explain what?" she broke in, anger replacing her former shock. "That you're a liar? That you only struck up a friendship with me because of the money? That's right, isn't it? Isn't that really what you've been after all along? Who are you working for, anyway? The bank the money was stolen from?" Willow asked, curiosity getting the better of her.

"Yes. I was hired to find the money after FBI and police efforts failed," Steven reluctantly admitted. He paused, wondering whether to tell her everything. Aware that she had him dead to rights, anyway, he added, "But I wasn't hired by the bank. I've been working for Addison Clayton since shortly after Cassie's conviction."

"But...Brad and Addison denied knowing you...." She recalled something else: Steven's presence at the ranch on the day of Cassie's death, his absence from her memorial service. What had seemed strange to Willow at the time was beginning to make a great deal of sense. Why would Steven have gone to Cassie's service when he was only a paid employee of her father's? As Willow slowly digested Steven's surprising announcement, a thought suddenly occurred to her; it narrowed her eyes and caused her voice to drip with suspicion.

"Tell me, did you really know Cassie? Or was that just another of your lies?" Steven was standing a few feet away from her, and Willow glared at him across the separating distance.

"No, I never had that pleasure. Everything I knew about her and about your relationship with her I learned from Addison Clayton. He wanted my working for him kept under wraps for reasons of his own," Steven confessed, his tone filled with intense regret. "Willow, I—"

Willow cut through his explanation. "But I told Addison the day Cassie died that I didn't know anything about the damned money. So why come after me?" No sooner had she framed the query than she knew the answer. Instantaneously, red-hot fury supplanted her anger.

Willow was now so enraged that she was shaking all over, her face contorted with emotion. "You thought I lied about it. Both you and Addison. That I intended to keep the money for myself! Right?" Instead of responding, Steven stood looking at her in silence. "Well, didn't you?" She hurled the accusation at him.

"Well...you have to admit two million dollars would be pretty tempting to anyone," Steven countered when at last he replied. "Especially if Cassie told you and you were the only one who knew where it was.

But that was in the beginning. I don't think now that you lied. I haven't since the kidnapping. You've got to believe that. It's the truth.''

Steven's eyes pleaded for understanding. But Willow was not in the least mollified. Addison's having doubted her integrity was infuriating, but Steven's having believed her a greedy, grasping liar cut to the quick. The wound ran so deep that she felt raw, lacerated, flayed. ''Thanks a hell of a lot! Is that supposed to make everything all right?'' She flung the question at him, trembling so savagely that she felt as though an earthquake had entered her body.

''No...I guess not....'' Steven conceded hesitantly. ''But I think if you had been in my position, you'd have thought the same thing. You were the one Cassie trusted the most, the last person she saw before she died. So it seemed logical that if she did tell anybody where the money was, it would have been you. As I said, though, I don't believe now you knew anything about it. I was only doing my job, you know,'' he added, trying to make her understand things from his perspective.

Willow was far too incensed to give it even the slightest consideration. She was interested only in the fact that he had deliberately deceived her and the elaborate lengths to which he'd gone to achieve that end. Thinking about them, she recalled phoning his office to verify his employment and asked, ''How did you get the woman I talked to to lie for you? And why the charade, anyway? If you believed I knew something about the money, why didn't you just ask me?''

No sooner had the words left her lips than she guessed the reply. It was glaringly apparent. If she had known Steven was a private investigator, and if she had been lying about the money, any such question would have put her on her guard.

Steven said, ''I've met with some resistance when people know my true profession, so I don't always mention it. In your case I didn't because I thought if I gained your confidence, you might accidentally let something slip. As to the real estate job, the receptionist is the wife of a close friend. She agreed to say I worked there so I could maintain my cover. Look, Willow. I know you're mad as hell, and I guess I can't really blame you. But—''

''Mad! Ha! If I were a man I'd thrash you within an inch of your life! You've lied to me! Thought I was a greedy grasping bitch! You've betrayed my trust! My I—'' Willow was so beside herself with hurt and rage that she almost blurted out her love for him. She caught herself only just in the nick of time.

''Is sleeping with the women involved in your cases one of the fringe benefits of your job? Does it include searching suitcases, skulking around people's houses at night? For a while I thought maybe it was Fielding, but I realize it could just as easily have been you. What a sleazy way to make a liv—'' Willow stopped, tears stinging the back of her throat and choking her so that she couldn't go on.

''I wasn't lying when I said I hadn't done those things. I'd already left the ranch when your suitcase was searched, but I'm pretty sure it was Addison Clayton who did it. I don't know anything about the prowler. Maybe it was Fielding, maybe it wasn't. I've admitted I gravitated to you because of my investigation into the money. But I was strongly attracted to you right from the start. God knows I fought hard enough against it, but I've really come to care for you. Please, Willow. Just let me hold you, show you I'm telling the truth.''

Steven moved toward her, his face full of entreaty, but Willow was beyond listening. The tears scalding the back of her throat were rapidly gathering in her eyes, but she refused to give him the satisfaction of seeing her cry. She swiftly eluded him with a backward step. Her voice tremulous, her eyes blazing, she said, ''Don't waste your time. I wouldn't believe anything you said! Just get out of here! I never want to see you again!''

Steven stopped, his outstretched arms falling to his sides. A muscle in his right cheek began to twitch, and whereas his eyes had held a plea for understanding, now they were smoldering with sudden anger.

''Okay. If that's the way you want it, I'll let it go for now.'' Steven's voice was a terse whisper. ''But if you ever cool off and decide to listen to reason, I'll be around.'' With that he grabbed the jacket he'd tossed over the back of a chair and stalked out.

The instant the door closed behind him, Willow dissolved in a crumpled heap on the sofa. The tears she had forcibly suppressed gushed forth and streaked down her cheeks. Harsh racking sobs of mingled pain and fury convulsed her slender body, and she didn't even try to stop them. So immersed was she in her turbulent emotions that she wasn't aware at first of a perceptible dampness on the sofa beneath her head. When she realized she was crying into the precise place where Steven's wine had spilled, she jumped to her feet, her explosive, "Dammit to hell!" shattering the hush in the room.

Her earlier efforts had done little to efface the red stain, and she rushed into the kitchen for the liquid spot remover she'd once used on Steven's suit coat. She scrubbed viciously at the smear, hoping that once it was eradicated, every trace of Steven would be eradicated, as well. She knew that ejecting him from her heart would not be accomplished quite so easily; the bitter knowledge made her scrub the sofa even more furiously.

When she had finished cleaning the couch, Willow carried the spot remover and cloth into the kitchen, and by the time she returned to the living room she had her emotions fairly under control. But rage erupted in her again when the doorbell chimed. She stomped to the door and jerked it open. "What're you still doing here? I told you to—" Her shrill voice came to a grinding halt when she spied Eileen on the porch.

Willow gaped at her, the turbulence of her emotions making her slow to grasp the fact that it was Eileen and not Steven. In the next instant uneasiness gripped her. Involuntarily her hand started to swing the door shut, but Eileen blocked the swing and pushed her way inside.

She looked at Willow's ravaged face in the dim light that filtered into the entry hall from the living room.

"My God, sweetie," Eileen said, concern in her hazel eyes, "you look terrible. Has something else happened?"

"I . . . no. . ." Willow's only thought was to get rid of Eileen as quickly as possible. Just seeing Eileen made Willow uneasy, and the realization that there was no one within earshot made her heartbeat accelerate to an alarming rate.

"Oh, come on. Something's obviously happened. Your eyes are all red and swollen and your face is blotchy. Tell me what it is," Eileen pressed her. She moved to close the door as she spoke. Despite the sharp blast of cold air it let in, the idea of having the door closed increased Willow's apprehension still more.

"No, please! Leave it open. I—I'm hot."

Eileen shot her a strange look but complied. Willow knew from the obstinacy in her face that Eileen wouldn't leave until an explanation for Willow's apparent distress had been extracted. Short of throwing her out bodily, there was really nothing she could do to make her leave.

Willow tried to think of some convincing falsehood but at first nothing came into her head. Then all at once a thought struck her. A private investigator was the closest thing to a policeman. If indeed Eileen were the culprit, the knowledge of Steven's identity might intimidate her, make her think twice about trying anything else. Without going into detail about how she had found out, Willow told her Steven's true profession.

"A private investigator . . . ?" Eileen echoed after a long pause. "Why would he lie about something like that? What difference does it make what he does, anyway?"

"He's been working for Cassie's father, trying to locate the money from the armored-car robbery. He thought I knew something that might lead him to it and passed himself off as a real estate agent so I wouldn't get wise to what he was up to. He was wasting his time, naturally. I have never known anything about the money,'' Willow added, carefully pronouncing each word. She watched Eileen closely for her reaction, but saw only sympathy stamped in her features.

''I don't blame you one bit for being upset with him for lying like that. I'd be furious, too. But you know, the times I've seen you together, it sure looked like he felt something for you. I can see you're really gone on the guy. Is there any chance you'll get over being mad and patch things up?''

Had Willow been speaking to anyone else, her answer would have been a resounding no. She purposely let a yielding note slip into her tone. ''I...maybe. We'll see.''

Eileen gave her a knowing smile. ''I think you're too hung up on him to stay mad for very long. Listen, honey, I came over to find out how your poor throat was. And to see if you have a box of pudding or Jell-O I could borrow. My crazy stomach's still hurting, and I thought something soft might help. I meant to check on you sooner, but I spent most of the weekend flat on my back in bed. Never mind all that now, though. I could stay with you for a while till you're feeling better, if you like.''

Eileen made the offer with what sounded like such genuine sincerity that Willow again thought she was going to feel just awful if Eileen was actually innocent of any wrongdoing. Since she had no way of knowing the truth, she declined. ''I'm not in a very good mood and I'd really like to be alone, if you don't mind. I think I've got a box of pudding I can let you have. My throat's feeling much better, but I'm sorry to hear your ulcer's still acting up. I didn't know you had one,'' Willow couldn't resist adding. A second later she could have bitten out her tongue, because if Eileen had guessed she was suspicious of her, wouldn't the remark be seen as proof?

Evidently not, for she responded nonchalantly, "I don't talk about it because I don't like to bore my friends with it. I just hate it when people go on about their health problems. It's a real drag." Eileen wrinkled her nose disdainfully.

The explanation sounded simple enough. Yet it was an enormous relief to see Eileen out after giving her the box of pudding.

When she had made certain the door was locked securely behind her, Willow traipsed back into the living room and plopped disconsolately into the cushioned rocker. Trixie emerged from the bedroom and sidled up to her, evidently in need of reassurance. Willow scooped the dog up in her arms and murmured soothing words into the furry ears.

Almost at once Trixie snuggled against her, relaxed and contented. Willow envied the dog's contentment. She could almost have wished that she hadn't discovered Steven's deception. That she could have gone on in blissful ignorance, basked in the warm glow of her newfound love forever. She knew the foolishness of this desire; she would have found out the truth sooner or later and the hurt she was feeling now would have been all the more painful.

Willow pondered everything Steven had said. He had accused Addison of searching her suitcase. Because she'd thought of Addison herself at the time, she owned that there could just possibly be some merit in Steven's accusation; she knew how desperate he was to find the missing money, and he might have thought she'd slipped something connected with it into the case. Regardless of Steven's denial about his being the prowler, though, she didn't know whether to believe him. If in fact he had been lurking in the yard, why couldn't he also have been responsible for the theft of Cassie's letter and the attempted theft of the doll-house?

Willow had been too overwrought to think about the break-in when she was railing at Steven only a while before or even when Eileen had been with her. Nor, since Steven seemed to have had nothing to gain by stealing the letter or the dollhouse, had she given any consideration to the possibility that he could have done it. Perhaps Eileen really was innocent, Steven the guilty one—not that Willow would have expected him to admit as much had she thought to confront him with it. He was such a master at fabrication that he would probably have lied about that, too.

Lies. Everything about him was a lie.

The ugly word stalked Willow when a couple of hours later she went to bed. A fruitless gesture. Her angry hurt and shattering sense of betrayal combined to make her too restless to sleep. She tossed and turned most of the night, then went to work Monday morning dull eyed, listless and unutterably depressed. The latter emotion stemmed from the grim knowledge that in spite of his painful deception, she would go on loving Steven for the rest of her life. She wished fervently that she could hate him, but she couldn't muster the negative emotion no matter how hard she tried.

This added to her depression and made her even more miserable.

Deputy Haggerty phoned Willow's office during her midmorning break with the results of the fingerprint tests on the extension cord and the dollhouse. Those on the cord had been too smudged to yield anything useful. The fingerprints on the little house were her own, Steven's, Eileen's and Fielding's—everyone who had been fingerprinted by the police earlier.

In regard to Fielding, the deputy informed her, "Except for his arraignment a couple of days after his release, he hasn't been seen around here since. His trial's been set for next month, by the way. But getting back to what I was saying, we also checked in Pleasanton, California, where he lives. According to his relatives and neighbors, he hasn't left the area. It's roughly two hundred and fifty miles away. So it'd be doggone hard for him to be gone the length of time it would take him to get here and back without somebody noticing he was gone."

Willow thanked him and hung up with a pensive frown. Because of the logistics involved, she reasoned that Deputy Haggerty could well be correct. The realization that she had nothing further to fear from Fielding came as a welcome relief, but there remained the question of who had attacked her. Who had stolen Cassie's letter? Who had tried to take the dollhouse? Steven? Willow's thoughts were interrupted when she was summoned to his chambers by the judge in whose courtroom she was working to discuss something in reference to the trial over which he was presiding.

HER ABJECT MISERY kept her awake for the second night running. She rose on Tuesday morning feeling even more listless than she had the day before. Fortunately, things at the courthouse ran smoothly, but because she knew that she'd have only her misery for company at home, she decided to work late that evening. Willow transcribed notes until seven, at which time her brain became so fuzzy from lack of sleep that she was forced to leave her office.

It was drizzling lightly when she stepped outside, and she lifted the collar of her winter-white coat as she trudged wearily along the darkened sidewalk. The long lonely evening stretched ahead of her. In spite of everything he had done to her, she missed Steven so much that the gnawing ache of his absence was a physical agony. She'd wondered if he would make any attempt to contact her, but he hadn't, and she didn't know whether to be glad or disappointed. She admitted to herself that the latter far outweighed the former, still one more fact that increased her wretchedness.

The cool drizzle of rain on her face failed to rouse her, but she was shocked into awareness when, as she started to cross the street a couple of blocks from home, a car suddenly shot out of nowhere and came roaring straight at her. She froze in midstride, impaled by the blinding glare of its high-beam headlights. Her blood surged to her head and crashed against her skull. The car bore unerringly down on her, its headlights the glowing eyes of a ferocious animal bent on devouring her.

It was only a few feet away now. With an adrenaline rush born of fear, Willow hurled herself at a pickup parked at the curb and rolled over its hood, to land on the sidewalk with a bone-jarring jolt that knocked the breath out of her lungs. She lay gasping, too stunned to move, her body twitching spasmodically. Her heart was pounding so violently that it almost blotted out the sound of screeching tires as the car sped away. Muffled footsteps on the sidewalk came rushing in her direction, and an elderly man trotted up to her.

"That damned fool nearly knocked you down! You all right, miss?" he asked as he bent over her. Willow was still so stunned that she could only nod. "Think you can stand up?" She nodded again, without really knowing if she could until he helped her gently to her feet. Her legs were trembling, her heart racing, but miraculously she was unharmed. With a shake of his grizzled head, he said, "You're a mighty lucky young woman. That jerk got so close, I thought for sure he was gonna get you."

"Then . . . you saw what happened . . . ?" Willow asked, when her shock had subsided enough to enable her to speak.

"I sure did. I live over there." He pointed to a nearby house. "I came out to get my cat and seen you crossing the street and the car coming down practically on top of you. Got a real good look at it, too. It was a honey of an old car with fancy grillwork. A black Jaguar."

Chapter Sixteen

A black Jaguar. The old man's words lashed Willow with the force of a whip. The brutal impact buckled her legs, and she reached out to grasp the man's arm. "I...er...it's d-dark, a-and couldn't you be mistaken?" She spoke through lips stiff with shock. As she had phrased the question, she noticed he was wearing thick glasses and prayed that his imperfect sight had caused him to make an error.

With implacable conviction, he repeated, "It was a black Jaguar, all right. I have a collection of model antique cars. I'd know a classic Jaguar anywhere. Got one in my collection. Didn't see the driver; I was too far away. And, like you said, it's dark. I'll tell you something, though. The dumb jackass don't deserve to have a honey of a car like that. Reckless driving, not watching where he's going, almost bowling decent people over. Say, miss, you sure you're okay?" the elderly gentleman inquired as he belatedly noticed Willow's stunned condition. "I think I'd better see you home."

The reaction that was setting in made Willow's legs shake so badly that she wasn't certain she could go the rest of the way on her own power. "Thank you. That's very nice of you. I'd really appreciate it." He proffered his arm, she took it gratefully and they moved together along the sidewalk through the drizzling rain.

It was only when Willow started walking that she became aware that her right hip was hurting. It had come down hard on the snow-packed ground. Her rescuer carried on a constant commentary about his model antique car collection, but his voice was only a droning buzz in Willow's ears. She was still trying to come to terms with the astonishing realization that it had been Steven's car that had nearly run her down.

At her house, she thanked the man for his kindness, and he saw her safely inside. Trixie greeted her with her old exuberance, but if Willow returned the greeting she wasn't conscious of it. She stood trembling, her back pressed against the front door, trying to absorb what had happened.

The elderly gentleman was clearly of the opinion that a reckless driver had nearly caused an accident. But the driver of the car had made no attempt to avoid Willow. Quite the reverse. He had deliberately launched the vehicle at her as if it were a guided missile, she its target. That the car was a black Jaguar couldn't possibly have been a coincidence; she doubted there was another like it in the state, let alone in Carson City.

But why had Steven attempted to run her down? Granted, she had been furious with him for his deception, for his having suspected she had lied about the money and intended to keep it. By the time she had finished railing at him, Steven had become angry himself. But surely not angry enough to try to injure—perhaps even kill—her.

Willow couldn't begin to fathom his reasons because there simply were none, at least none she was aware of. She knew only that things were becoming more frightening all the time. The thought of Steven's deliberate attempt to harm her was too shattering, too incredible to believe. Yet he had. The knowledge of her love for him stuck in her throat.

She went into the kitchen to telephone the sheriff's office, rubbing her painful hip. She reported the attempted hit-and-run, then asked the man to whom she spoke to send out a patrol car as quickly as possible.

"Sorry, ma'am. I can't do it. Two-thirds of our manpower's out with the flu," he informed Willow apologetically. "What few available units we've got are out. Even so, we're answering all calls according to their priority. So it will be quite a while before they get to yours. Maybe you should come down and make a report instead."

"Yes, thank you. I will," Willow agreed. The instant she hung up the phone, a sudden unsettling thought caused her to change her mind, however. What if Steven was lurking somewhere outside, watching, waiting for another chance to get at her? No. Better to remain behind the relative safety of locked doors and make her report in the morning.

With that decision, Willow shrugged out of her coat, noting for the first time the dark smudges of dirt, the deep rent in the side panel. The hood ornament on the pickup truck must have caught it. The coat was ruined beyond repair. Her nylons were tattered, soiled. She felt grimy. Her body was still shaking from reaction. Her hip was beginning to throb.

Running hot water into the tub, she wished she could soak away the desolating knowledge that Steven had tried to run her down. The wish only served as a reminder of Friday's incident.

When she'd realized that Steven could well be responsible for it, she hadn't really considered the various factors involved. Now, climbing into the tub, she considered them. Steven had had access to the dollhouse on numerous occasions, so if he suspected it contained something connected with the money and had wanted to examine it, he could have done so at any time—unless he had been unable to because of Willow's presence in the house. As for Cassie's letter, the same applied, which could have been the reason he'd sneaked into the house when he was sure Willow wouldn't be there. Aside from Eileen, he knew Willow's daily routine better than anyone else.

Another idea cropped up that she hadn't considered before, either. If Steven was the guilty one, his actions in no way resembled those of the private investigators Willow had seen depicted in films and on TV. Just the opposite. Theft, burglary, assault, perhaps even attempted murder—behavior surely beyond the boundaries of his profession, more befitting someone with an extremely violent nature. Or a criminal mind.

Willow's hand stopped in midmotion as she reached for the soap.

The third person in the armored-car robbery.

Willow had of course previously suspected it had been Eileen. She suddenly began to wonder if, incredible as it seemed, Steven could have been that unidentified accomplice. She'd heard of a few rare instances where honest policemen became corrupt, so why couldn't the same thing happen to a private investigator? Steven seemed to have plenty of money, and Willow had always assumed that part of his income was from his silent partnership in his family's hotel chain. But was the largest portion of his income in reality from illegal sources? Oh, God. Not Steven. Willow's heart rejected the notion, but her brain obstinately clung to it.

Her bathwater had begun to cool. Willow climbed out of the tub, more reflections crowding her mind as she dried herself off. She remembered Steven's having admitted he'd never really known Cassie, but realized this might be yet another of his lies. If in fact he was the unknown accomplice in the robbery, he would have been acquainted with her. Further, he could have accepted the assignment to investigate the disappearance of the money with the intention of finding and keeping it for himself. And he'd had the unmitigated gall to confess that he had thought Willow unscrupulous!

She knew that her sickening speculations about Steven were merely speculations, perhaps preposterous ones. But they continued as she padded into the bedroom and put on her nightgown and robe. Steven had questioned her about whether she thought the dollhouse and Cassie's letter contained some sort of

clue. He'd been quite persistent, she recalled, and even
the police seemed to think it was a possibility.

Because of her firm conviction that Cassie was ig-
norant of the location of the money, Willow had
scoffed at the idea. She was still persuaded that she
was right. But what if she wasn't? Could she risk
something else happening without trying to find out
if Steven's apparent belief had any basis in fact?

Willow knew she could not. She had to explore
every possibility, regardless of how remote it seemed.
Trixie was sitting in front of her dish, a pointed reminder that it was a couple of hours past her supper-
time. Willow murmured, "Okay, in a while," on her
way into the dining room. There she switched on the
light and turned the dollhouse sideways so that she
could open the double doors at the rear. Her gray eyes
narrowed in keen concentration, she slowly examined
all four rooms. Also, whereas she'd given only cursory thought to the letter when the police had inquired about it, now she tried to recall everything
Cassie had said.

She remembered only snatches of it. Cassie had
written about the dollhouse, about Willow's prison
visits, her own progressive weakness caused by her illness. Whether Willow's memory lapse was due to the
fact that she'd only read the letter once, to her lack of
sleep, or the unnerving realization that Steven had
tried to harm her, she wasn't sure. So she returned her
attention to the dollhouse once more. She noticed
nothing out of the ordinary. The lovely little structure
looked so innocent that Willow couldn't help but

wonder ruefully how it could pose such a dangerous threat.

She studied it until a whining sound from Trixie drew her back into the kitchen. Willow fed the dog, then though she herself didn't feel hungry, she warmed a bowl of soup to quiet her stomach. She'd eaten nothing since noon.

Spooning in the soup, she remembered the ferocity with which Steven had fought Fielding on the night of the abduction, his solicitude for her afterward, the tender way he had made love to her for the first time after Friday's attack. Ironic memories now, considering the reprehensible things Willow suspected Steven of having perpetrated.

Puzzling, too, was his rescuing her from Fielding only to assault her, then perhaps try to kill her himself shortly after. Steven had been so quick to point the finger of guilt at the prison guard. Had he done so to make himself appear innocent? Was the rage he'd directed at Fielding a ruse to enable him to play the indignant lover?

But if Steven had wanted to hurt her, why hadn't he tried when they were at his cabin? He'd certainly had ample opportunity, yet he had waited until tonight. Why?

As she put her bowl into the dishwasher, Willow ruminated on the question. But she couldn't answer it any more than she could understand the reason for Steven's actions this evening. The most important thing at the moment was to prevent any further attacks from occurring; Willow knew she might not survive another. And if indeed the dollhouse held part of the secret that would solve the puzzle of the missing money, she had better find out what it was, and quickly. Willow retraced her steps into the dining room, an expression of obstinate determination on her face.

She scrutinized the dollhouse even more closely than she had before. She started with the top floor, pausing to open the door of the tiny Franklin stove with one finger to see if something was secreted inside. There wasn't. So her scrutiny moved down to the second floor. She examined everything in the master bedroom, felt underneath the bed in case anything was hidden beneath the bedspread. Again nothing.

Next she looked in the nursery, removing the small strip of linen from the wooden cradle on the slim chance that there was something under it. Once more with the same results. She then checked everything in the first floor parlor, and lifted the lid of the minuscule sewing table to study the various compartments. Then, when this also yielded nothing, Willow got a magnifying glass from a drawer in the maple hutch and carefully read the postage-stamp-sized newspaper the tiny man on the settee was holding to see if it contained a message. It didn't.

It had begun to rain in earnest now, heavy raindrops spattering on the roof, high winds whipping at the windows as if the storm were trying to escape the havoc of its own creation. Willow ignored the sounds. Her eyes still lingering on the furnishings in the parlor, she concentrated again on the contents of Cassie's letter. At first she recalled only the few items she had recalled before. Then she remembered Cassie's explanation about giving her the dollhouse to replace the one that had been destroyed and Cassie's thanks for her loving care. But that was all. Surely, though, there was nothing of any import in these messages, nor in the dollhouse. Willow was beginning to think that her painstaking search was an exercise in futility.

Despite her growing conviction, she went on peering into the parlor. Her impatient gaze wandered to the petit-point sampler on the wall, the matching oval rug on the floor. Both showed a brown well and a brown bucket against a white background. Willow had noticed them before, of course. Since Cassie had been good at petit point, she assumed they were her handiwork. She marveled anew at the intricacy of the minute stitches. Still, she saw nothing of any significance in either of these and started to turn away with a disgusted sigh.

Then, as if floodgates in her mind had suddenly opened, she remembered Cassie's letter mentioning The Alamo, the original ranch house on the Clayton property where the girls had played as children. The old dry well and oaken bucket in the courtyard of the ranch house. Momentarily, Willow recalled Cassie had written about the numerous relationships she'd had in her life: she'd had so many that if they had been grains of sand, they would have filled a bucket....

"Oh, my God," Willow whispered, unconscious that she had spoken or that her eyes were as big as saucers. Could the petit-point sampler and rug, Cassie's mention of The Alamo, the word *bucket* in her letter all be clues to something that would lead to the money? Could she have hidden something in the bucket of the old dry well at the abandoned ranch house? Or were all these things only a series of unrelated coincidences?

Willow didn't think so. She realized now that Cassie must have known all along where the two million dollars were. What Willow couldn't comprehend was why she had gone to such lengths to conceal the money.

Willow pulled out a chair and sat down to contemplate the matter. It crossed her mind that perhaps Cassie had wanted to make restitution of the money through her to prevent Addison from taking credit for its recovery. Willow had suspected that he hoped to find it himself to impress the public and his political constituents before reentering the political arena— which, she reasoned, was why he had hired Steven. For if Steven had found the money, Addison would have undoubtedly been the one to return it to the bank from which it had been taken. It came to her also that Cassie might have feared that the third participant in the robbery would attempt to locate the two million dollars, another reason for her using references in her letter that only Willow would understand.

Willow realized that her thoughts about Cassie's reasons were speculation, but she was reasonably certain that she had solved the riddle of the missing money. She decided to keep her theory to herself, at least until she had proof to substantiate it. The only way to do that, of course, was to go to the abandoned ranch house to examine the bucket and the well.

She was tempted to drive to Reno then and there, but she rejected the idea, afraid Steven might be loitering somewhere outside. She resolved instead to go in the morning after she had gone to the sheriff's office to report the attempted hit-and-run. If she found anything, and she was almost certain that she would, she would take it promptly to the police.

Willow wished it were morning already. To make the hours pass more quickly, she puttered around the house for a while, then curled up in the wing chair with a book. Owing to the excitement of her discovery and the distress of the attempt on her life, she doubted she would get any rest. The lack of sleep she'd had the past two nights caught up with her, however, and she drifted off to sleep sitting up, the book falling in her lap. She was wakened rudely by a sharp rapping on the front door some time later.

Willow started, her brain foggy, her sleep-glazed eyes traveling to the digital clock on the VCR. It was ten-fifteen. She stood, surprised to find she had been sleeping for almost two hours. She wondered groggily who could be knocking on the door so late. Even as she did so, there came another insistent rap, this with unmistakable urgency. Willow remembered her phone call to the police, and thinking they had sent out a patrol car after all, she hurried into the entry hall. She snapped on the porch light and looked through the peephole.

Contrary to Willow's expectations, it wasn't the police. It was Steven. As she spied him, her heart skidded to a sudden stop, and she took a swift backward step, uncertain about what to do. She wished she hadn't turned on the porch light, that she had pretended to be asleep and hadn't heard him. But it was too late. Steven knew she had.

In confirmation, he called to her, his terse voice as urgent as his rapping. "Willow? It's me, Steven. Let me in."

Naturally, nothing could induce Willow to open the door to him. But still she stood there, irresolute. She remained silent, quivering with apprehension, but was forced to respond when Steven repeated his command. "I...it's late. What do you w-want?" she quavered, her heart in her mouth.

"I know it's late. But we've got to talk. Open up and let me in."

"No! I—I have nothing to say to you. So just go away!"

Willow shrank against the wall, hoping her command would send him on his way. She started violently as Steven retorted sharply, "Well, I've got something to say to you. Look, I know you're probably still mad, but we've got to talk. Get this thing settled once and for all. Tonight! Are you going to let me in, or do I have to break the door down to get to you?"

Insistent before, Steven's voice was all at once impatient, angry, fraught with relentless determination. Willow wasted no time in considering what he meant. Only too clearly it was she he wanted to finish! Did he really believe she was crazy enough to obey his command? If so, he had another think coming! Abrupt anger warring with apprehension, she wondered what he would do if she confronted him with her suspicions. Not that she intended to; she was too afraid of him. The thought was thrust from her mind a moment later when Steven began to rattle the doorknob.

Her voice shrill with sudden panic, Willow shouted, "I told you to go away! So get out of here. Now!" Almost at once the knob stopped turning and Steven grew so quiet that Willow wondered if he had gone. Hope sprang up again as she tiptoed to peer out the peephole, only to die when she saw that Steven was still there.

He was staring at the door, a dark scowl quirking his brow, a calculating expression on his face, as if he were mentally testing the strength of the lock. Willow looked out at him, almost too afraid to breathe. Then with a savage, "Damn!" he turned and stalked off the porch, anger visible in every inch of him. Willow watched his retreating back until he was swallowed up by the darkness, her sigh of relief hissing in her throat. She stayed where she was, listening for the sound of his car engine. Then when she heard him drive away, she sped to the window nearest the street to make sure he didn't circle the block and come back.

When several minutes elapsed and she saw no sign of his car, she hastened into the kitchen to call the police again. The fact that Steven hadn't returned didn't mean he wasn't planning to, and Willow wasn't about to take any chances. Her hand shaking, she dialed the sheriff's number, was answered by the man she had spoken to before, and identified herself as the person who had reported the hit-and-run attempt. This time she named Steven as the perpetrator, related his visit and expressed her fear that he might return.

"Well, ma'am, I'm sorry to say things have worsened here. Three more men down with the bug, so God only knows when I can get a unit there. I know you're scared, but just try to be calm, make sure everything's locked up tight and don't open the door if this guy shows up again—"

Willow's customary good manners deserted her and she hung up in the midst of this unnecessary advice. She was shaking, and tears of fear, anger and frustration gathered in her eyes. How could she be calm when Steven might come back at any minute? She hadn't seen or heard from Eileen in the past couple of days, but now that she no longer considered her a threat, she decided to call her to alert her to the situation. She got no answer, and it was frighteningly obvious that she would have to defend herself if Steven tried to get in.

Since Willow had nothing else with which to protect herself, she took the largest butcher knife she had out of its drawer. The prospect of using it on Steven both sickened and frightened her, yet she knew she would have to if he forced her into it. Revulsion and grim resignation mingling with the sudden nausea that knotted her stomach, Willow carried the knife into the living room, then settled in a chair to wait.

STEVEN DOWNSHIFTED to negotiate a sharp corner, almost scraping the tires against the curb. He was too angry to care. Willow's hostile attitude had left him with no choice but to get the hell out of there, to let things ride for the time being. He had no intention of giving up, though. There was too damned much at stake to let it all slip through his fingers, more at stake than Willow realized. But he was determined somehow to get to her if it was the last thing he ever did.

Chapter Seventeen

Morning dawned dismal and gloomy, but Willow embraced it as if it were the sunniest of mornings. The night just past had been the longest, most grueling and nerve-racking she had ever spent. She was exhausted from her all-night vigil, yet profoundly relieved, as well. In spite of her terrible fear, Steven hadn't come back, nor had there been any sign of the police.

After dressing quickly, she telephoned another court reporter to cover for her for the entire day. She wasn't sure precisely when she would return from Reno, and afterward she intended to come home and catch up on some much needed rest.

Willow gathered up her purse and heavy parka and moved through the quiet house to the front door. As she stepped outside, she cast an apprehensive glance around for Steven's car, but it was not there. Feeling enormously relieved, she climbed into her Camaro.

Although the storm had abated, dark clouds cloaked the sky like a murky gray shroud, and Willow switched on her headlights as she backed the car out of the driveway. She kept an eye out for Steven during the short drive to the sheriff's office, but there was no sign of him.

The building was quiet, and not many men were around—apparently the result of the flu outbreak. Willow told one of the deputies the reason for her visit, and he led her into a side room. There she was introduced to another officer, to whom she reported the attempted hit-and-run. She gave him Steven's name and spelled it out as he wrote down the information.

"This Mr. Randall. You say he deliberately tried to injure you. Do you know why?" The officer peered at her across the desk, his eyes squinting in the dim overhead light.

"No, but I—" Willow was about to relate the things she suspected Steven of having done, but realized that in spite of her suspicions she really had no proof of his guilt. "No. I just know he did. He drives a classic black Jaguar, and I'm fairly sure there isn't another one like it anywhere around here."

"Classic Jaguar. Steven Randall." The officer stopped writing, his expression pensive. "The name sounds familiar, and now that I think about it, so does the car. Hang on a minute. I'll be right back." He strode out of the room and was gone for several minutes. When he returned, he said, "I thought so. Mr. Randall called last evening to report the vehicle stolen."

Willow found it strange that Steven would report the car stolen after purposely using it to run her down—unless it was a clever maneuver to give him an air of innocence. Either that, she mused, or Steven knew the elderly man had seen his Jaguar and decided he'd better do something about it. Or...could it be, Willow wondered with a small spark of hope, that he was really innocent?

She wished with all her heart that she could believe in his innocence, but there were too many things against him. The feeble spark of hope was extinguished like a match in a strong gale as the officer broke into her thoughts. "We'll get hold of Mr. Randall and bring him in for questioning. Do you know where he lives?"

Though Willow had never been to Steven's condominium, he had given her the address shortly after they had started dating on a regular basis. She supplied the officer with it, signed the requisite statement form, then climbed back into her car for the half-hour ride to Reno.

She kept watch for the black Jaguar through her rearview mirror as she drove, but there was no evidence of it. The highway was teeming with early morning traffic, and Willow was forced to drive more slowly than she would have liked. As she turned off the highway onto the road that fronted the ranch, she decided against stopping there to tell the Claytons of her theory. Her decision was founded on the premise that if in fact she found anything, Addison would probably try to take credit for its discovery, and if her speculations were correct, Cassie hadn't wanted that.

Having passed the ranch, Willow turned onto a side road that led to the original ranch house. It was a narrow dirt track, wide enough for only one vehicle, the rain-melted snow making it muddy and slick. Once more she was forced to go slowly. She proceeded along the road until it gave way a couple of miles later to wild plant life, which had been allowed to grow un-checked over the years.

Aware that she would have to go the last half mile or so on foot, Willow got out of the car, her shoes sinking deeply into the slushy, snow-crusted mud. The stunted manzanita and creosote bushes springing up all around her shivered in the stiff wind that blew across the open terrain. The keening noise they made blended with the mournful howl of a coyote some-where in the distance, and Willow experienced an urge to shiver herself at the unpleasant sound.

She picked up her pace, as her head lowered to keep the wind out of her face. But her steps slowed, then came to a complete stop when a sudden prickly sen-sation crawled up her spine. She felt as though she were being watched. Willow turned sharply to look around, trepidation coursing through her as she scanned the landscape. She saw nothing unusual and set the creepy feeling down to an onslaught of ner-vousness, annoyed with herself for having let her imagination run as wild as the tangled plants jutting up in her path.

She lengthened her stride, conscious that she was trespassing. She felt sneaky, surreptitious, but squelched this feeling, too, assuring herself that her infringement was absolutely necessary under the cir-cumstances. Still, she was glad when the adobe wall that encircled the old ranch house loomed into view.

The adobe was chipped, and the wall itself leaned drunkenly, eroded by the ravages of time and neglect. Recollections of the happy hours she and Cassie had whiled away there surfaced in Willow's mind, but were replaced by sadness as she stepped through an arch-

way in the wall to find the Spanish-style ranch house
in a similarly run-down condition.

The roof sagged, and portions of the walls were
badly crumbled; the shutters swung on rusted hinges.
Willow paused briefly to look at the house. The Alamo had always seemed a friendly place, but now, in
the gloomy light of this overcast day, it looked somber, eerie, almost menacing. Suddenly anxious to get
away from this place of so many fond childhood
memories, Willow went over to the brick well in the
center of the courtyard.

The oaken bucket was lowered into the well, and she
swiftly pulled it up. Her heartbeat accelerated as she
spied a small metal container wrapped in a plastic bag
at the bottom of the bucket. She discarded the plastic
bag, opened the container and discovered what appeared to be a key to a safety-deposit box inside. A
tingle went through her. Written in Cassie's hand-
writing on a slip of paper under the key was the name
of a savings-and-loan company in nearby Truckee, on
the California-Nevada border.

Willow guessed Cassie had put the two million dollars in the California savings-and-loan company because she hadn't wanted to risk being recognized
nearer to home, where she was well-known. Willow
was enormously excited about her discovery but suddenly frightened about it, as well, because she knew
that if the wrong person ever learned about what she
had found, she would be in more danger than ever.
Steven?

She banished the thought of him. More anxious
than ever to get away and to put what she'd found into
the capable hands of the police, she returned the slip

of paper to the container, along with the key, and stowed them in her shoulder bag. She was about to turn from the well when suddenly a voice behind her said, "I had a feeling if I stuck to you, you'd lead me to the money. And you have, haven't you?"

Willow started violently, her frightened yelp gurgling in her throat. Mike stood a few feet away, blocking her path, a pistol in his hand. An amused grin wreathed his angular features as she stared at him, the shock of seeing him there rendering her brain slow to register the significance of his words. When at last they sank in, Willow gaped at him in astonishment. How could she have been so stupid? Why had she never considered Mike before, yet had suspected everyone else—including Steven?

"You...?" she whispered, the word snatched away by the wind. That feeling of being watched hadn't been nervous imagination; Mike must have been following her. Mike had been the third person in the armored-car robbery. Not Steven after all. Willow felt the relief of that knowledge while not ignoring the reality of the gun in Mike's hand. "You were the other accomplice in the robbery." She made her words a statement.

"Right," Mike readily agreed. He grinned again as if amused.

"But Cassie—how did—"

"How did she get involved?" he cut in, anticipating her question. "She horned in. Norris and I were in a bar one night planning the heist." Norris was the man who had died during a prison riot. "Cassandra Clayton was sitting in the next booth and overheard us. She demanded to be let in and threatened to blab to the cops if we didn't let her. We separated after the job, she with the money 'cause Norris and I couldn't decide who'd keep it till we met to divide the take a few days after the heat died down. Norris and me, that is. She didn't want the money. Said she was in it for the thrill, but I always had a feeling there was more to it than that. Anyway, those two jerks went and got caught before we could meet to split the dough," Mike added derisively. "but she must've hid the money for safekeeping before that."

The discovery of Mike's true identity—and her previous blindness to it—was beginning to wear off. With its abatement, a surge of renewed fear enveloped Willow, the sour taste of it filling her mouth. She was alone with him in these deserted ruins, miles from the nearest form of civilization, too far away for anybody to hear if she screamed for help. She cast a covert glance around, calculating her chances of bolting and making a run for it. But they were enclosed by the adobe wall, and Mike moved to stand closer. She doubted she would get a foot away before he caught her. He seemed in a garrulous mood, and she decided to keep him talking until she could think of some way to escape.

Striving for a curious tone so that he wouldn't comprehend what she had in mind, Willow commented, "But I had nothing to do with the robbery. So what made you think I was connected with the money?" Mike shifted position, and she forcibly steeled herself against recoiling. Despite her effort to sound curious, her voice came out shrill, but if he noticed, he chose to ignore it.

He responded readily again. "I read a local magazine article about how Cassandra Clayton's family and her dear childhood friend, Willow Laughlin, visited her in prison. It talked about her being sick, too. It was obvious her family and the cops didn't know where the money was or it would've been reported. I figured she'd tell somebody about it, though. She was dying, and I thought she'd want to get it off her chest. You were her best friend, and I figured if she told anybody, it would most likely be you. I looked you up, moved to Carson City, and followed you around till I learned your routine. It seemed to me that if you knew about the money and planned to keep it, you wouldn't be dumb enough to have it in the house. But I thought there might be something there telling where it was. I've been searching your place for quite a while now."

So here was someone else who thought Willow unscrupulous and greedy. Her fear became tempered with anger, but instinct warned her against displaying her emotions. Mike's having searched her house without her knowledge gave her an eerie, violated feeling; but it made her genuinely curious, too. "There was never any sign of forced entry. How did you get in?"

"I used a credit card. They don't just work in the movies, you know." Mike grinned again, and it occurred to Willow that she had never noticed how false, how furtive, his smile really was. Sweet, friendly, Mike. Not sweet at all, but phony, sly, deceitful.

Mike continued. "You didn't make it easy on me, though. Leaving the lights and TV on whenever you were gone. That's why I always called before one of my little hunting trips."

By now Willow had realized that Mike had been the prowler she'd encountered in her backyard. She remembered how he'd rushed to her defense that evening, his Good Neighbor Sam act when he had fixed her flat tire, his shocked concern on the night of the kidnapping. She remembered his amusement during the presumed obscene telephone call.

As if he read her thoughts, he remarked, "I liked that bit about my reaching the sheriff's house. That was funny." He chuckled as he had done that evening on the telephone, the sinister quality of his mirth sending a shiver along her back.

Willow darted another surreptitious glance around, hoping desperately that someone would come along. Futile hope, she knew. They were completely isolated from the rest of the world; the weather was cold and blustery. Who would be coming out to this godforsaken place on such a dismal day?

She tried to keep her voice calm. "I'm still curious. Was it you who attacked me? And did you steel Cassie's letter and try to take the dollhouse?" She wanted to hear his confession from his own mouth, as well as to stall for time.

"Right on all counts. The letter wasn't any help at all, and neither was the dollhouse. I found out about it from Eileen, naturally. It was really handy living with her. I learned a lot about you from her, even though it was you I'd planned to make a play for the first time we met. I engineered the whole thing, only you were hung up on that lawyer, so I had to settle for Eileen instead. Like I said, she came in real handy."

Mike smirked so mockingly that in spite of the violence she knew him capable of and the nerve-tingling fear she felt at being trapped alone with him, Willow wanted to slap his face. Poor Eileen. She had been his unwitting dupe, and very likely didn't realize it even now.

Until then Mike had seemed affable, amused, but suddenly he grew serious. "I saw you put something in your purse a few minutes ago. So why don't you be a nice girl and hand it over." Aware that she had no option but to obey, Willow unzipped her shoulder bag, her hand hesitating on the opening as she tried frantically to think of something inside the bag that she could use as a weapon against him. Fingernail file, comb, compact. Mentally she ticked off the contents of the bag, then gave a guilty start when Mike said in a menacing growl, "Don't even think of doing anything stupid or you'll be sorry." For emphasis, he leveled the gun straight at her heart.

Terror replaced fear, and Willow broke out into a cold sweat. Rivulets of perspiration trickled down her back, and her hands were wet, clammy. Mike's expression was as threatening as his voice; he looked as if he might pull the trigger at any second. Willow knew she had to do something to divert his attention, but what? She said the first thing that popped into her head. "O-okay. I—I'll give it to you. But I'd like to know why you tried to run me down. It was you, wasn't it?"

Willow licked terror-parched lips as she waited for him to reply. He took so long that she thought he intended to shoot her instead of answering. When at last he spoke, he was impatient, surly.

"I don't see what difference it makes now. Yeah, it was me. I was sure you saw me in the closet the other

day. I couldn't let you get away to tell the cops, 'cause
if they knew I'd tried to snatch that stupid dollhouse,
they might just have put two and two together and
linked me to the robbery. Which would've been bad
for me. I'm wanted in Florida for the same thing. Only
under my real name. I'd have finished you off and
saved myself a helluva lot of trouble if Eileen hadn't
come barging in.

"I've been hiding out ever since and waiting for
another chance at you. I'd have had it when you and
Pretty Boy Randall went to his place in Tahoe. Right."
Mike smiled again at Willow's unconcealed surprise.
"I followed you two there, but your watchdog Randall stuck to you like glue, so I couldn't do anything."

He was talking freely again, so Willow asked, swallowing past the lump of terror in her throat, "But
what about Eileen? Didn't she wonder where you
were?" *Please God. Let somebody come,* she prayed
desperately.

With a derision that filled her with disgust, Mike
said, "That broad's so gullible, she'd believe anything I told her. I trumped up some story about having to go out of town on an emergency. But the
suspense of not knowing what the hell was going on
got to me. So I called her. She told me about somebody attacking you, but didn't say anything about the
cops looking for me. I knew I'd done a pretty good job
on you with the extension cord and I figured maybe
the shock temporarily blocked your mind or something. Only I couldn't afford to take any chances.
Even though I'd gone through hell to get that damned

money, I wasn't about to go to prison. Now cut the gab and give me what you've got in your purse.''

Willow's hand was still hovering on the opening of her bag. She reached inside, found the metal container and drew it out. Mike stared at it, his expression one of pure greed. Murderous intent glittered in his tawny eyes, and she said through terror-numbed lips, ''I can see why keeping out of prison was important to you. But Steven's car—why did you use it to try to kill me?''

''Dammit, you're as nosy as that gumshoe boyfriend of yours! He asked a lot of questions, too, the first time I met him. Said I looked familiar, wanted to know where I was from and such. The bastard even went snooping around the car lot where I work. Asked the boss all about me. I already knew he was curious about me, and that made me nervous as hell. Specially when Eileen told me the other night he was really a private eye. So I decided to kill two birds with one stone. Get rid of you and use pretty boy's fancy set of wheels to do it. Pin the rap on him for snooping around about me. That's all I'm gonna say. Hand the box over! Now!''

On the barked command Mike moved closer still, cocked the hammer of his gun, then trained it on Willow's heart again. She stared at the pistol in horrified fascination, aware that the instant she complied, he would shoot her.

The well was only a foot or so behind her. With a quick sidestep she pivoted and hurled the metal container into the well.

Simultaneously Mike lunged to intercept it, his finger on the trigger jerking to fire a shot that whizzed past Willow's shoulder. With a scream, he plunged headfirst into the well. The scream was abruptly cut off, and except for the howling wind, there was only silence.

Chapter Eighteen

Willow stood rooted to the spot in mingled shock and horror, her ears still ringing from the shattering reverberation of the gun. She had come so near to death that she was slow to grasp the fact that she was alive. Every nerve in her body twitching, her legs so rubbery that she could scarcely move, she inched to the well and called down to him. No response. Mike was dead or unconscious. Knowing that she had to tell someone what had happened, she turned and ran back the way she had come as fast as her wobbly legs would carry her.

Willow slipped and slid, the muddy slush impeding her progress. When she finally reached her car, she paid no attention to Mike's, parked alongside it, but climbed into her Camaro to drive to the ranch for help. Before she could start, a blue station wagon drove up and screeched to a stop beside her.

Steven jumped out of the station wagon and ran to open her door. He demanded, "Are you all right? What happened? What are you doing out here?"

"I'm okay. But . . . Mike . . . he . . . the well. He fell in . . . he . . . I think he's dead," Willow gasped, breathless from running, her words coming out in a disjointed rush. Steven understood her nonetheless. He told her to scoot over, and he slid behind the wheel. He drove in silence until Willow had caught her breath, then he said, "Now tell me what happened."

Willow told him about the clues in the dollhouse, those in Cassie's letter, and the metal box she had found in the bucket of the well and the paper bearing the name of the savings-and-loan company. "I'm positive the robbery money's there. But I threw the box into the well. Mike wanted it—he was going to kill me. He was the one who attacked me and stole the letter. He was the other accomplice in the robbery." Willow paused, still finding this fact almost too incredible to believe. "Mike Peters isn't his real name. He's a wanted criminal. He—"

"I thought I recognized him from someplace," Steven broke in, unsurprised. "I got to wondering about him, so I did some checking around. Never found out anything, though. Probably because I was looking under the wrong name. Never did figure out where I'd seen him before, but it must have been a wanted poster or something."

"He told me. About your asking questions about him. He was going to kill me the day he tried to steal the dollhouse, because he thought I'd seen him in the utility closet. He stole your car last night and tried to run me down with it. He was going to frame you for investigating him." It was only then that it occurred to Willow to wonder what reason Steven had had for driving out to the old Clayton house, but the ranch sprang into view just then, and she set her curiosity aside for the time being.

Opal Andrews let them in and allowed Steven to use the phone to call the authorities. According to Opal, Brad and Addison were away on business, Jennifer at school. Opal ushered them into the living room to wait for the police. While they waited, Willow voiced her curiosity.

"The police called last night to say they'd found the Jaguar unharmed a few hours after I'd reported it stolen," Steven explained. "When I left your house I drove around, debating whether or not I should go back and force you to let me in. I'd been thinking about what had happened and I knew the dollhouse and the letter *had* to have some connection with the money. It was the only thing that made sense. That's why I insisted you let me in and why I got so mad when you wouldn't. I knew whoever attacked you wasn't going to let up and you were in terrible danger. But I couldn't do anything without your cooperation. I knew you were probably still angry with me for lying to you, but you acted scared to death of me," he added ruefully.

"I was. I thought you'd tried to run me over," Willow admitted, the long fearful night she'd spent waiting for Steven to return still fresh in her mind. "I even imagined you might have been the third person in the robbery," she added, feeling silly now that she had suspected him.

"What! Oh, God. No wonder you wouldn't open the door." Steven grew quiet a moment, thinking about her confession. Then he continued. "Anyway, after I left your place I drove around for a while. Even circled your block once, and when I did, I spotted Mike parked on the opposite corner. He ducked when I drove past and obviously didn't want to be seen. It was obvious, too, that he was watching your house. He couldn't see Eileen's from where he was. Naturally, that made me curious. So I decided to keep an eye on him. I knew my Jag would stick out like a sore thumb, so I beat it to the airport and rented the station wagon. Then I parked and watched Mike watch your house all night."

Belatedly Willow noticed the dark stubble on his chin and his bloodshot eyes, evidence of his all-night vigil. The knowledge that he hadn't been guilty of the horrid things she'd suspected him of salved the angry hurt caused by his deception. She wanted to go to him, to stroke the weariness from his beloved face, but she felt awkward and embarrassed. Would it ever be right between them?

Steven continued. "This morning, when Peters followed you to the sheriff's office, I tailed you both, and on to Reno. By then I knew, of course, that he was up to no good, and I finally figured out that he had to have been the one who'd attacked you. I kept a safe distance so that he wouldn't spot me. Then when traffic got thick just outside town, I lost sight of him. I guessed from the direction you'd taken that you were headed for the ranch. But when I got here I didn't see any sign of your cars. So I drove around like crazy, then when I saw tire tracks on the dirt road, I followed."

Steven halted and passed a hand over his eyes. His gut wrenched as he relived those hellish fear-ridden minutes when he'd driven around frantically looking for Willow and Peters. God, he'd never forget them if he lived to be a hundred. Dropping his hand to his side, he murmured, his voice thick, "Willow, we've got to talk. To straighten this thing out between us. But I guess it'll have to wait till the Peters business is over." He sighed heavily at the sound of approaching sirens.

At Steven's suggestion, Willow waited at the ranch while he accompanied the police to the abandoned ranch house. After what seemed a decade but was in reality twenty minutes or so, he returned along with three policemen.

"His arm's broken and he's got a concussion, but he'll be able to stand trial," one of the officers informed Willow. Another siren, this evidently the ambulance taking Mike away, punctuated his words. "We retrieved the metal box Mr. Randall says contains a key to a safe-deposit box you think holds the money from the robbery Miss Clayton was involved in. We've got a man on his way to the savings-and-loan company in Truckee right now. Mr. Randall shares your opinion about the money being there, and if it is, a lot of people are going to be glad this thing has finally been resolved. I need some information from you about what happened. And we'll need a formal statement from you at the station."

Once more Willow answered questions and supplied the police with everything they needed to know. She was exhausted when she finished, but intensely heartened that her terrifying experiences were behind her. She would have to testify at Fielding's trial and then Mike's, after which, she hoped, her wish to resume a normal life would at last be realized.

Steven drove her to the Reno police station, where she signed a statement. They had left her Camaro at the ranch; Steven promised to get it later. They were both quiet during the drive back to Carson City, their thoughts revolving around the events of the morning.

Trixie greeted Steven as a long-lost friend when they entered the house and curled up at his feet when he seated himself beside Willow on the sofa.

Tension stretched between them. It was heavy, almost a tangible thing. Though Steven had wanted to discuss their situation before, now he was somber, uncommunicative. Discomfited, Willow searched for something to say to ease the strained atmosphere, yet she found herself oddly tongue-tied and shy. She had never experienced anything like it before but guessed that Steven was as ill-at-ease as she.

Finally, after what seemed an eternity, Steven ended the silence by remarking, as if he'd only just now thought of the matter, "You never said what you were doing at the sheriff's office."

"Oh, that. I stopped by to report the attempted hit-and-run. I gave the police your name and address, I'm afraid. They're probably looking for you right now. I—I'm sorry, but I didn't know..." Willow flushed with embarrassment.

"It's okay. I'll clear it with them. How were you supposed to know it was Peters and not me?"

"I didn't. But speaking of Mike, I don't think Eileen knows what's happened. I'm going to have to break it to her. Poor thing, she's going to be so upset. He was only using her and she really cared for him." The unbearable tension had subsided at last, and Willow gave a relieved sigh.

"I'll help you break the news to her. It'll be upsetting, but I don't think you need to worry too much about Eileen. She strikes me as a survivor. She'll get over it. What about you? Can you forgive me for lying to you the way I did? I thought it was a necessary part of my job, and at first it didn't bother me. But then I realized I loved you and I've never felt so lousy about anything in my life. I was so afraid you'd hate me if you knew the truth."

"I was outraged. Not only because you'd lied, but because of your thinking I was such a scheming witch. That really hurt. I did try to hate you, only I couldn't. And I guess I'm going to have to forgive you or go on being miserable," Willow murmured ruefully.

"Thank God." Steven released his breath gustily. "Will you give me a chance to make it up to you? Convince you I really love you? I do, my darling, more than I ever thought it possible to love anyone. I want to spend the rest of my life with you. Will you marry me?"

Willow's shyness fled, and her heart sang with joy. Her face radiant with the glow of love, she whispered, "Yes, oh, yes. I'll marry you, my love. I—"

Steven smothered her words as his mouth swooped down to cover hers in a long, passionate kiss from which they both emerged breathless, shaken. He cradled Willow gently in his arms, and they held each other, both reveling in their love. After a time Steven murmured wryly, "It's a good thing you forgave me. If you hadn't, I would have hounded you until you finally gave in. I wasn't about to let you go that easily."

"I'm glad I did, too. But if you ever deceive me in any way again, I want you to know there will be hell to pay," Willow warned him, with a tremulous smile.

Steven kissed her again, and a long, satisfying silence ensued. He broke it, suddenly troubled. At Willow's inquiring look, he said, "I feel badly about not being able to help Addison Clayton. He paid me an excellent fee, but you were the one who solved the puzzle of the missing money. Some P.I. I am, huh?"

"Just because you didn't solve the case doesn't mean you aren't a great detective," Willow quickly assured him with a loving smile. "But I can't really feel too sorry for Addison. Now that the two million dollars have been found, he'll probably go back into politics and go on being his old manipulative self. I'm so glad Cassie made restitution of the money, though. She was the only real loser in all this. Poor Cassie. How terrible for a child and parent to have so much resentment for each other. When we start our own family, I'm going to make sure nothing like that ever happens with our kids. You won't let it happen, either, will you?"

To dispel the sadness for Cassie's misspent life that dimmed the love light in Willow's eyes, Steven asserted confidently, "That's something you'll never have to worry about. I promise, my darling." He framed her face with his hands and sealed the solemn pledge with a tender kiss.

Take 4 best-selling love stories FREE
Plus get a FREE surprise gift!

Janet Dailey
Americana

A romantic tour of America with
Janet Dailey!

Enjoy two releases each month from this
collection of your favorite previously
published Janet Dailey titles, presented
alphabetically state by state.

Available NOW wherever paperback books
are sold.

Explore love with Harlequin in the Middle
Ages, the Renaissance, in the Regency, the
Victorian and other eras.

Relive within these books the endless ages of
romance, set against authentic historical
backgrounds. Two new historical love stories
published each month.

HIST-A-1